Jo's Boys

LOUISA MAY ALCOTT

Adapted by Bob Blaisdell
Illustrated by Natalie Carabetta

DOVER PUBLICATIONS, INC.
Mineola, New York

DOVER CHILDREN'S THRIFT CLASSICS
GENERAL EDITOR: PAUL NEGRI
EDITOR OF THIS VOLUME: JOHN BERSETH

Copyright

Copyright © 1999 by Dover Publications, Inc.
All rights reserved under Pan American and International Copyright Conventions.

Published in Canada by General Publishing Company, Ltd., 30 Lesmill Road, Don Mills, Toronto, Ontario.

Bibliographical Note

This Dover edition, first published in 1999, is a new abridgment of a standard text of *Jo's Boys*. The introductory Note and the illustrations were prepared specially for this edition.

Library of Congress Cataloging-in-Publication Data

Alcott, Louisa May, 1832–1888.
    Joe's boys / Louisa May Alcott ; [abridged by] Bob Blaisdell ; illustrated by Natalie Carabetta.
        p.   cm. — (Dover children's thrift classics)
    "This Dover edition, first published in 1999, is a new abridgment of a standard text of Joe's boys. The introductory note and the illustrations were prepared specially for this edition"—T.p. verso.
    Sequel to: Little men.
    Summary: Recounts the further adventures, successes, and failures of the numerous young men of Plumfield school.
    ISBN 0-486-40789-6 (pbk.)
    [1. Boarding schools—Fiction. 2. Schools—Fiction. 3. Family life—New England—Fiction. 4. New England—Fiction.]   I. Blaisdell, Robert.
II. Carabetta, Natalie, ill. III. Title. IV. Series.
PZ7.A335Jo   1999
[Fic]—dc21   99–32233
                                                        CIP

Manufactured in the United States of America
Dover Publications, Inc., 31 East 2nd Street, Mineola, N.Y. 11501

Contents

Note

LOUISA MAY ALCOTT (1832–1888) was one of four daughters of the philosopher and educator Amos Bronson Alcott. She lived most of her life in and around Concord, Massachusetts. Her father was an innovative thinker but an impractical man, filled with idealistic plans that did little to support his family. Louisa was educated by her parents and by family friends such as Henry David Thoreau and Ralph Waldo Emerson. As a teenager she was obliged to work in domestic service and as a teacher to supplement the family income. But she spent much of her time writing, especially plays, short stories, and sensational thrillers. Magazines began to print her work, and in 1860 one of her stories was published in the *Atlantic Monthly*. Early in the Civil War she served as a volunteer nurse in Washington, D.C.

In writing *Little Women* (1868–1869), her first children's book, Alcott drew on her childhood experiences, modeling the characters of the March girls upon herself and her sisters. The book's instant success freed the Alcotts from their financial difficulties and won the author recognition and acclaim; it was to be the first in an enormously popular series. The present volume, written in 1886, follows Meg, Amy, and especially Jo (Beth has died) into middle age, as they attempt to guide their children through the joys and trials of early adulthood. Far from being solely about the "boys," this is also the story of the strong, ambitious, and (typical of Alcott) highly principled young women of Plumfield.

1. Ten Years Later

"If anyone had told me what wonderful changes were to take place here in ten years, I wouldn't have believed it," said Mrs. Jo to Mrs. Meg, as they sat on the piazza at Plumfield one summer day, looking about them with faces full of pride and pleasure.

"This is the sort of magic that money and kind hearts can work. I am sure Mr. Laurence could have no nobler monument than the college he so generously endowed; and a home like this will keep Aunt March's memory green as long as it lasts," answered Mrs. Meg.

"We used to believe in fairies, you remember, and plan what we'd ask for if we could have three wishes. Doesn't it seem as if mine had been really granted at last? Money, fame and plenty of work I love," said Mrs. Jo.

"I have had mine, and Amy is enjoying hers. If dear Marmee, John and Beth were here, it would be quite perfect," added Meg.

Jo put her hand on her sister's, and both sat silent for a little while, looking out over the pleasant scene before them. It certainly did seem as if magic had been at work, for in the years since Jo and Meg had been girls, quiet Plumfield had become a busy little world. The house was bigger and in better shape than it had been when riotous boys swarmed everywhere. On the hill, where they as children used to fly their kites, stood the fine college which Mr. Laurence's generous donations of money had built. Busy students were going to and fro along the paths

1

the women knew as girls, and many young men and women were enjoying all the advantages that college could give them.

Just inside the gates of Plumfield a pretty brown cottage nestled among the trees, and on the green slope westward Laurie's white-pillared mansion glittered in the sunshine.

Mr. Bhaer was now president, and Mr. March, the Little Women's father, was chaplain of Laurence College. The sisters divided the care of the students among them, each taking the part that suited her best. Meg was the motherly friend of the young women, Jo was the defender of all the youths, and Amy the Generous helped the needy ones, and entertained them all in her home so graciously that it was no wonder they named her home Mount Parnassus.

The original twelve Little Men had of course scattered far and wide during these years, but all that lived still remembered old Plumfield, and came wandering back from the four quarters of the earth to tell their various experiences. I will tell a few words of each, and then we can go on with the newest chapters of their lives.

Franz, one of Professor Bhaer's German nephews, a man of twenty-six, was with a merchant kinsman in Hamburg, and doing well. Emil, the other German nephew, was the jolliest sailor that ever "sailed the ocean blue." His uncle sent him on a long voyage to disgust him with this adventurous life; but he came home so delighted with it that it was plain this was his profession, and a German kinsman gave him a good position in his ships; so the lad was happy. Dan, the troubled, good-hearted, restless boy, was a wanderer still; for after doing geological research in South America, he tried sheep-farming in Australia, and was now in California doing mining. Nat, the violinist, was busy at a conservatory of music in nearby Boston, preparing for a year or two in Germany to finish off his training. Tommy Bangs was studying medicine and trying to like it. Jack was in business with his father. Dolly was in college

with Stuffy and Ned, training to be a lawyer. Poor little
Dick was dead, so was Billy.

Meanwhile, Jo's sons were called "the Lion and the
Lamb"; for Ted was a king of beasts, and Rob was as gentle as any sheep. Rob was a dutiful child, but in Ted Mrs.
Jo seemed to see all the faults and fun of her own childhood in a new shape. He had his moods of gloom, but patient Rob and his mother knew just when to let him alone
or to shake him up. He was her pride and joy as well as
torment, being a very bright lad for his age, and so full of
all sorts of budding talent that Mrs. Jo thought much
about what this remarkable boy would become.

Demi, Meg's son, had gone through college with honors,
and Mrs. Meg had set her heart on his becoming a minister. But John, as she called him now, firmly declined the
divinity school, saying he had had enough of books, and
needed to know more of men and the world, and caused
the dear woman much disappointment by deciding to be
a journalist. It was a blow; but she knew that young minds
cannot be driven, and that experience is the best teacher,
so she let him follow his own inclinations.

The girls were all flourishing. Daisy, as sweet and domestic as ever, was Meg's comfort and companion. Josie,
at fourteen, was a most original young person; she had a
passion for acting, which caused her quiet mother and
sister much worry as well as amusement. Bess, Amy's
daughter, had grown into a tall, beautiful girl, looking several years older than she was. But the pride of the com-
munity was Naughty Nan; for, like so many restless, wilful
children, she was growing into a woman full of the energy
and promise that suddenly blossoms when she finds the
work she is fitted to do well. Nan began to study medicine
at sixteen, and at twenty was getting on bravely; for now,
thanks to other intelligent women, attendance at colleges
and work in hospitals were open to her. She had never wa-
vered in her purpose from the childhood days when she
shocked Daisy in the old willow by saying, "I don't want
any family to fuss over. I shall have an office, with bottles

and tools in it, and drive round and cure folks." This prophecy of the future was coming true; and as she was finding so much happiness in it, nothing could win her from her chosen work. Several worthy young gentlemen had tried to make her change her mind and choose, as Daisy did, "a nice little house and a family to have and take care of," but Nan only laughed, and dismissed the would-be husbands. Only one refused to be put off.

This was Tom Bangs, who was as faithful to his childhood sweetheart as she was to her medical training. He studied medicine for her sake alone, having no taste for it. But Nan was firm in her refusals to wed, and they remained, in spite of their quibbling over her unromantic feelings, excellent friends.

Both were approaching Plumfield, one after the other, on the afternoon when Mrs. Meg and Mrs. Jo were talking on the piazza. Nan was a handsome girl, with clear eyes and a quick smile, and the self-poised look young women with a purpose always have. She was simply and sensibly dressed, walked easily, and seemed full of vigor, with her broad shoulders well back, arms swinging freely. The few people she met turned to look at her, as if it was a pleasant sight to see a hearty, happy girl walking countryward that lovely day; and the red-faced young man steaming along behind, hat off, trying to catch up to her, must have agreed with them.

Soon his "Hello!" got her attention, and Nan paused, and said, "Oh, is that you, Tom?"

"Looks like it. I thought you might be walking out today."

"No, you *knew* I would. So how is your throat?"

"My throat?—Oh, ah, yes, I remember. It is well. The effect of those pills you gave me was wonderful."

"O Tom, Tom—there was nothing in them but sugar and flour. Will you never be done playing your tricks?"

"O Nan, Nan, will you never be done seeing through them?"

And the merry pair laughed just as they did in the old times.

Soon his "Hello" got her attention,
and Nan paused, and said, "Oh, is that you, Tom?"

Tom went on to say, "Well, I knew I wouldn't be able to see you for a week if I didn't come up with some excuse for a call at your office. You are so busy all the time I never get to talk to you."

"You ought to be busy too, and above such nonsense. Really, Tom, if you don't give your all to your studies, you'll never get on as a doctor."

"I can't study all the time," answered Tom. "Though some people seem to be able to."

"Then why not leave medicine and do what suits you better?"

"You know why I chose medicine, and why I shall stick to it even if it kills me. I have heart trouble, you know, and only one doctor in the world can cure it—but she won't!"

Nan frowned. "She is curing it in the best and only way; but a more difficult patient never lived. Did you go to that ball, as I ordered?"

"I did."

"And did you devote yourself to pretty Miss West?"

"Danced with her the whole evening."

"And your heart didn't recover its strength?"

"Only you can get it to do that, Nan."

"You silly men think we must pair off as we did when we were children; but we shall do nothing of the kind.—Oh, how fine Parnassus looks from here!" said Nan, changing the subject.

"It is a fine house," said Tom, "but I love the old Plumfield best."

A sudden whoop startled them, as a tall boy with wild blond head came leaping over the hedge like a kangaroo, followed by a slim girl, who got stuck in the hedge and sat there laughing. She was a pretty little lass, with curly dark hair, bright eyes and expressive face.

"Help me out, Nan, please! Tom, hold Ted; he's got my book, and I want it back," called Josie from her position in the bush.

Tom promptly collared the thief, while Nan picked up Josie from among the thorns and set her on her feet.

"What's the matter, dear?" asked Nan, examining the scratches on the girl's hands.

"I was studying my part, and cousin Ted came up and poked the play out of my hands. It fell in the brook, and before I could scramble down he was off with it. You wretch, give it back this moment or I'll box your ears!" cried Josie, laughing and scolding in the same breath.

Escaping from Tom, Ted began reciting from the play in a ridiculous but funny way.

The sound of applause from Jo and Meg on the piazza put a stop to these antics, and the young folks went up the avenue together. Breathless and merry, they greeted the ladies and sat down on the steps to rest. Aunt Meg began sewing up the fresh tears in Josie's dress, while Mrs. Jo petted Teddy and rescued the book. Daisy appeared in a moment to greet her friend Nan, and all began to talk.

"Any news of the commodore?" asked Tom.

"Emil is on his way home," answered Mrs. Jo, "and Dan hopes to come soon. I long to see my boys together, and have begged the wanderers to come to Thanksgiving, if not before."

"They'll come, every man of them, for the sake of our jolly old dinners," said Tom.

"If Nat leaves us at the end of the month," said Nan to Daisy, "we shall have to have a farewell party for him."

A blush came into Daisy's cheek, but she answered calmly, "Uncle Laurie says he has real talent, and after the training he will get abroad he can earn a good living here, though he may never be famous."

"Young people seldom turn out as one predicts, so it is of little use to expect anything," said Mrs. Meg. "If our children are good men and women, we should be satisfied; yet it's very natural to wish them to be brilliant and successful."

"They are like my chickens, mighty uncertain," said Ted with a laugh.

"I want to see Dan settled somewhere. At twenty-five he

is still roaming about the world without a tie to hold him, except Jo," said Meg.

"Dan will find his place at last, and experience is his best teacher. He is rough still, but each time he comes home I see a change for the better, and never lose my faith in him. He may never do anything great, or get rich; but if the wild boy makes an honest man, I'm satisfied," said Mrs. Jo.

"That's right, mother," said Ted. "Stand by Dan! He's worth a dozen Jacks and Neds bragging about money and trying to be swells. You see if he doesn't do something to be proud of."

"He's just the fellow to do rash things and come to glory," said Tom Bangs. "Perhaps his way is better than ours."

"Much better," said Mrs. Jo. "I'd rather send my boys off to see the world than leave them alone in a city full of temptations, with nothing to do but waste time, money and health. Dan has to work his way, and that teaches him courage, patience and self-reliance. I don't worry about him as much as I do about George and Dolly at college, no more fit than two babies to take care of themselves."

"How about our Demi-John? He's knocking round town as a newspaper man," asked Tom. "Speak of the devil! Here he is."

"Hot off the press! Commodore Emil is in the harbor, and will cut his ship cable and run before the wind as soon as he can get off," called Demi.

Everyone talked together for a moment, and a copy of John's newspaper was passed from hand to hand that each eye might rest on the pleasant fact that Emil, on the *Brenda,* from Hamburg, was safe in port.

"He'll come lurching out tomorrow with his usual collection of marine monsters and lively yarns," said John.

"And how's his brother Franz?" asked Mrs. Jo.

"He's going to be married! There's news for you. The first of the flock, Aunt, to do that, so say good-bye to him. Her name is Ludmilla Hildegard Blumenthal—German, of course. The dear old boy wants his uncle Fritz's consent, and then he will settle down over there to be a happy and an honest citizen. Long life to him!"

"I'm glad to hear it. I do so like to settle my boys with a good wife and a nice little home," said Mrs. Jo; for she often felt like a distracted hen with a large brood of mixed chickens and ducks upon her hands.

Tom sighed, with a sly glance at Nan, "Marriage is what a fellow needs to keep him steady; and it's the duty of nice girls to marry as soon as possible, isn't it, Demi?"

"If there are enough nice fellows to go round," answered John.

"It takes three or four women to get a man into, through and out of the world," said Mrs. Jo. "You are costly creatures, my boys. And it is well that mothers, sisters, wives and daughters love their duty and do it so well, or you would perish off the face of the earth."

"I am very glad, then," said Nan, "that my being a doctor will make me a useful, happy and independent spinster."

Mrs. Jo, laughing, said, "I take great pride in you, Nan, and hope to see you very successful; for we do need just such helpful women in the world. I sometimes feel as if I'd missed my calling and ought to have remained single."

"What should I ever have done without my dearest Mum?" asked Ted, giving her a hug.

Here Josie, who had been studying her part in a play at the other end of the piazza, suddenly burst forth with a shriek, and gave Juliet's speech in the tomb so effectively that the boys applauded.

"That child is a born actress," said Mrs. Jo to Meg.

"Now I know how dear Marmee felt when I begged to be an actress," said Meg. "I never can consent to her leading such a life."

Demi, hearing these words, went and gave Josie a shake, saying, "Drop that nonsense in public."

"Let me alone, boy, or I'll do the 'Maniac Bride,' with my best *Ha-ha*!" cried Josie. Dramatically proclaiming "Mrs.

Woffington's carriage awaits," she swept down the steps and round the corner, trailing Daisy's scarlet shawl behind her.

"Isn't she great fun? If she ever turns prim and proper, I'm leaving town; so mind how you nip her in the bud," said Teddy, frowning at Demi.

"You two are a team," said Mrs. Jo, "cousins though you are. Josie ought to have been your sister, and Rob Meg's child. Then your house, Meg, would have been all peace and mine all craziness. Now I must go and tell Laurie the news. Come with me, Meg, a little stroll will do us good." And sticking Ted's straw hat on her head, Mrs. Jo walked off with her sister, leaving Daisy to attend to serving the visitors some muffins.

2. Parnassus

It was well named, after the home of the temple of Apollo, god of the arts. And our old friend Laurie, as genial as ever, was a mature Apollo; time had ripened the boy into a noble man. Life had been sweet for Laurie and Amy since they married. Their house was full of beauty and comfort, and here the art-loving host and hostess attracted and entertained artists of all kinds. Laurie was a generous patron to musicians, while Amy had her protégées among young painters and sculptors. Their daughter Bess had grown old enough to share the joys and labors of art.

Jo and Meg went at once to the art studio, where mother and daughter were working together. Bess was busy with the bust of a little child, while her mother added the last touches to a fine head of her husband. Time seemed to have stood still with Amy, for happiness had kept her young and wealth had given her the culture she needed. It was evident that she adored her daughter, and well she might; for the beauty she had longed for seemed, to her fond eyes at least, to be impersonated in this younger self. Bess inherited her mother's beautiful figure, blue eyes, fair skin and golden hair, tied up in the same knot of curls. Also—ah! never-ending source of joy to Amy—she had her father's handsome nose and mouth. In the quiet studio with her mother, she worked away with the focus of a true artist, until Aunt Jo came in exclaiming, "My dear girls, stop making mud-pies and hear the news!"

Amy and Bess dropped their tools and greeted Jo and Meg. They were all in the full tide of gossip when, several minutes later, Laurie arrived and listened with interest to the news of Franz and Emil.

"The marriage bug has broken out," said Laurie, "and now it will infect your whole crew. Be prepared for every sort of romance, Jo."

"I know it, and I hope I shall be able to pull them through and land them safely."

With Meg getting up and going out of the room, Laurie said, "I'm afraid Meg won't be happy when our fiddling Nat begins to come too near her Daisy."

"Nat is a good boy," said Jo.

"But a poor one, and one yet to be proven by experience," said Laurie. "Come and have a cup of tea, old dears, and we'll see what the young folks are up to." And Laurie, staring at Jo and Amy, said he found it hard to realize that they ever had been little Amy and riotous Jo.

"Don't suggest we are growing old, my lord. We have only bloomed; and a very nice bouquet we make with our buds about us," answered Mrs. Amy.

"Not to mention our thorns and dead leaves," added Jo, with a sigh; for life had never been very easy to her, and even now she had her troubles both within and without.

They found Meg in the parlor, which was full of afternoon sunshine and the rustle of trees; for the three long windows opened on the garden. The great music-room was at one end, and at the other, a little household shrine, with portraits and sculpted busts of the departed family members: Marmee, Aunt March, John and dear, sweet Beth.

The three sisters stood a moment looking at the beloved picture of Marmee; for this noble mother had been so much to them that no one could ever fill her place. Only two years since she had gone away to live and love in heaven.

"I can ask for nothing better for my child," said Laurie, "than that she may be a woman like your mother."

Just then a fresh voice began to sing "Ave Maria" in the

music-room, and it was Bess, singing a song that reminded them all of Marmee, and they sat down together
near the open windows enjoying the music, while Laurie
brought the sisters tea.

Nat soon came in with Demi, then Ted and Josie, the
professor and his Rob, all anxious to hear about "the
boys."

Professor Bhaer was gray now, but strong and kind as
ever; for he had work he loved, and the whole college felt
his beautiful influence. Rob was as much like him as it was
possible for a boy to be, and was already called "the
young professor."

"Well, heart's dearest," said Mr. Bhaer, seating himself
beside Jo, "we will have our boys again."

"Oh, Fritz, I'm so delighted about Emil, and, if you ap-
prove, about Franz also. Is it a wise match?" asked Mrs.
Jo.

"Yes, I think so. But Franz is so German he will not live
here but stay in his fatherland."

"And Emil, he is to be second mate next voyage; isn't
that fine? I'm so happy both your nephews have done
well; you gave up so much for them and their mother,"
said Jo.

He laughed and whispered, "If I had not come to America for the poor lads, I never should have found my Jo."
The professor still considered his wife the dearest woman
in the world.

Nat approached at the beckoning of Mr. Bhaer, who
said, "I have the letters of introduction for you, my son.
They are two old friends of mine in Leipsic, who will
watch out for you. It is well you will have them, for you
will be heartbroken at first, Nat, and need comforting."

Nat was a man now, but he needed the stimulus of for-
eign training in music and the self-dependence of living on
his own. Indeed, it was for the sake of Daisy that Nat was
setting out. The cherished dream of his life was to earn a
place for himself as a musician and win this angel for his
wife.

Mrs. Jo knew this, and though he was not exactly the man she would have chosen for her niece, she felt that Nat would always need just the wise and loving care Daisy could give him, and that without it there was danger of his being one of the good-natured, aimless men who fail for want of the right pilot to steer them safely through the world. Mrs. Meg frowned upon the boy's love, and would not hear of giving her dear girl to any but the best man to be found on the face of the earth. "Nat was not man enough, never would be. No one knew his family, a musician's life was a hard one; Daisy was too young. Perhaps five or six years' time will prove him. Let us see what absence will do for him." And that was the end of it.

Mrs. Jo was thinking of Meg's words as she looked at Nat while he talked with her husband about Leipsic, and she resolved to have a talk with him before he went; for she talked freely with her boys about the trials and temptations that fall to us all.

Then it was that Mr. March, the little women's father, came in with several young men and women; for the wise old man was beloved, and as chaplain ministered to his flock. Bess went to him at once; for since Marmee died, Grandpapa was her special care, and it was sweet to see the golden head bend over the silver one as she rolled out his easy chair and waited on him.

Bess then sat on one arm of his chair, holding a glass of fresh milk. Josie came and perched on the other arm; she had been having a hot discussion with Ted, and had got the worst of it.

"Grandpa," she said, "must women always obey men and say they are the wisest, just because they are the strongest?"

"Well, my dear," said Mr. March, "that is the old-fashioned belief, and it will take some time to change it. But I think the woman's hour has struck, and it looks to me as if the boys must do their best, for the girls have caught up, and may reach the goal first." He looked about at the bright faces of the young women, who were among the best students in the college.

Josie replied, "Then I'll show Teddy that a woman can act as well, if not better, than a man. I'll never own that my brain isn't as good as his."

"If you shake your head in that angry way, you'll scramble what brains you have got; I'd take care of 'em, if I were you," teased Ted.

"What started this civil war?" asked Grandpapa.

"Why, we were reading the Iliad and came to where Zeus tells Hera not to ask about his plans, or he'll whip her, and Josie was disgusted because Hera meekly hushed up. I said it was right, and agreed with the old fellow that women didn't know much and ought to obey men," explained Ted.

"Goddesses may do as they like," argued Josie, "but those Greek and Trojan women were poor-spirited things if they listened to men who couldn't fight their own battles and had to be hustled off by Athena, Aphrodite and Hera when they were going to get beaten."

Everyone laughed at Josie's scorn of Homer and the gods.

"You can fight like a Trojan, that's evident; and we will be the two armies looking on while you and Ted have it out," said Mr. March.

"We will fight it out later when there are no goddesses to interfere," said Teddy, as he turned away to go after the treats.

"Conquered by a muffin!" laughed Josie.

As Josie chased after him out of the room, a dark-skinned young man in a blue suit came leaping up the steps with a cheery, "Ahoy! Ahoy! Where is everybody?"

"Emil! Emil!" cried Josie. And in a moment Ted was upon him and welcoming the newcomer.

Muffins were forgotten; and towing their cousin like two tugboats at a big ship, the children returned to the parlor, where Emil kissed all the women and shook hands with all men except his uncle; him he embraced in the good old German style.

"Didn't think I could get off today, but found I could, and steered straight for old Plumfield. Not a soul there, so I luffed and bore away for Parnassus, and here is every man Jack of you. Bless your hearts, how glad I am to see you all!" exclaimed the sailor boy, beaming at them, as he stood with his legs apart as if he still felt the rocking deck under his feet.

"You ought to 'shiver your timbers,' not 'bless our hearts,' Emil!—Oh, how nice and shippy and tarry you do smell!" said Josie, sniffing at him with great enjoyment of the fresh sea odors he brought with him.

This was her favorite cousin, and she was his pet; so she knew that the bulging pockets of the blue jacket contained treasures for her.

"Avast, my hearty, and let me take soundings before you dive into my pockets," laughed Emil, while holding her off with one hand and with the other he rummaged out odd little boxes and packages marked with different names, and handed them round: a necklace of pretty pink coral for Josie; a string of pearly shells in a silver chain for Bess; a brooch in the shape of a violin for Daisy. Emil joked, "I thought Daisy would like a fiddle, and Nat can find her a *beau*."

"I know she will," answered Nat, "and I'll take it to her."

Emil chuckled, and handed out a carved bear whose head opened, showing a deep inkstand. This he presented to Aunt Jo.

"Knowing your fondness for these fine animals," he joked again, "I brought this one to your *pen*."

"Very good, Commodore!" said Mrs. Jo.

"As Aunt Meg insists on wearing caps, in spite of being so young, I got her some bits of lace. Hope you'll like 'em." And out of soft paper came some filmy things, one of which soon lay like a net of snowflakes on Mrs. Meg's pretty hair.

"I couldn't find anything swell enough for Aunt Amy, because she has everything she wants, so I brought her a little picture that always makes me think of her when Bess

was a baby." He handed her an oval ivory locket, on which
was painted a golden-haired Madonna with a rosy child.

"How lovely!" cried everyone. And Aunt Amy at once
hung it about her neck on the blue ribbon from Bess's
hair, charmed with her gift; for it recalled the happiest
year of her life.

"I've got a lot of plunder for your fellows in my chest,
but I knew I should have no peace till my cargo for the
girls was unloaded. Now tell me all the news." And, seated
on Amy's best marble-topped table, the sailor swung his
legs and talked at the rate of ten knots an hour, till Aunt
Jo carried them all off to a grand family tea in honor of the
Commodore.

3. Dan

The March family had enjoyed a great many surprises in the course of their varied career, but the greatest of all was when the Ugly Duckling, Jo March Bhaer, turned out to be, not a swan, but a golden goose, whose literary eggs found such an unexpected market that in ten years Jo's wildest and most cherished dream actually came true. How or why it happened she never clearly understood, but all of a sudden she found herself famous in a small way, and, better still, with a snug little fortune in her pocket to clear away the obstacles of the present and assure the future of her boys.

It began in a bad year when everything went wrong at Plumfield; times were hard, the school enrollment dwindled, Jo overworked herself and had a long illness; Laurie and Amy were overseas, and the Bhaers were too proud to ask for help from their family. Confined to her room, Jo wrote a book for girls, hastily describing a few scenes and adventures in the lives of herself and her sisters. The public admired it, and this earned her a great deal of money.

The success Jo valued most was the new power to make her mother's last years happy and serene. As a girl, Jo's favorite dream had been to have a room where Marmee could sit in peace and enjoy herself after her hard, heroic life. Now the dream had become a happy fact, and Marmee sat in her pleasant chamber with every comfort and luxury about her, loving daughters to wait upon her as her disabilities increased, a faithful mate to lean upon, and grandchildren to brighten the twilight of life with affection. Marmee rejoiced as only mothers can in the good fortunes of their children.

On the other hand, Jo suffered from her fame. The admiring public took up her time. Strangers demanded to look at her, question, advise, warn, congratulate and drive her out of her wits by their attention. Jo's health suffered, but for a time she gratefully gave all of herself to literature for the young, feeling that she owed a great deal to the little friends in whose sight she found such favor. But the time came when her patience gave out.

"There ought to be a law to protect unfortunate authors," said Mrs. Jo one morning soon after Emil's arrival, when the mail brought her an unusually large and varied assortment of letters requesting advice, attention and autographs. She and Ted glanced through them, and then she set to work on a serial novel. She told the servant-girl, "Deny me to everybody, Mary. I won't see Queen Victoria if she comes today."

"I hope the day will go well with you, my dearest," said her husband, who had been busy with his own mail. "I will dine at the college with Professor Plock, who is to visit us today. The young ones can dine on Parnassus; so you shall have a quiet time." And smoothing the worried lines out of her forehead with his good-bye kiss, the excellent man marched away, both pockets full of books, an old umbrella in one hand and a bag of rocks for the geology class in the other.

"If all literary women had such thoughtful angels for husbands, they would live longer and write more," said Mrs. Jo to her spouse.

Rob started for school at the same time, looking so much like him with his books and bag and square shoulders that his mother laughed as she turned away, "Bless both my dear professors, for better creatures never lived!"

There were many interruptions through the day, and Mrs. Jo was despairing of ever completing her work. It was almost sunset when Mary popped her head into Jo's parlor to say a gentleman wished to see Mrs. Bhaer, and wouldn't take no for an answer.

"He must, because I shall *not* go down and see anyone. This has been an awful day, and I won't be disturbed again," replied the harassed author, pausing in the midst of the grand finale of her chapter.

"I told him so, ma'am, but he walked right in as bold as brass. I guess he's another crazy one, and I declare I'm almost afraid of him, he's so big and dark, and cool as cucumbers, though I will say he's good-looking," added Mary.

"My day has been ruined, and I *will* have this last half-hour to finish. Tell him to go away; I *won't* go down," cried Mrs. Jo.

Mary went, and Jo, listening in spite of herself, heard a murmur of voices, then a cry from Mary. Mrs. Bhaer flung down her pen and went to the rescue.

The intruder seemed to be storming the staircase, which Mary was gallantly defending.

"Who is this person who insists on remaining when I have declined to see him?" exclaimed the harassed author.

"I'm sure I don't know, ma'am. He won't give no name, and says you'll be sorry if you don't see him," answered Mary.

"Won't you be sorry?" asked the stranger, looking up with a pair of dark eyes full of laughter, the flash of white teeth through a long beard, and both hands out as he boldly approached the irate lady.

Mrs. Jo gave one keen look, for the voice was familiar; then completed Mary's surprise by throwing both arms round the brigand's neck, exclaiming joyfully, "My dearest boy, where did you come from?"

"California—on purpose to see you, Mother Bhaer. Now won't you be sorry if I go away?" answered the one and only Dan, with a hearty kiss.

"To think of my ordering you out of the house when I've

been longing to see you for a year," laughed Mrs. Jo, as
she went down to have a good talk with her returned
wanderer.

Mrs. Jo often thought that Dan had Indian blood in him,
not only because of his love of a wild, wandering life, but
his appearance; for, as he grew up, this became more
striking. At twenty-five he was very tall, with muscular
limbs, a keen, dark face, and the alert look of one whose
senses were all alive; rough in manner, full of energy,
quick with word or blow, eyes full of the old fire, always
watchful as if used to keeping guard, and a general air of
vigor and freshness very charming to those who knew the
dangers and delights of his adventurous life. He was looking his best as he sat talking with "Mother Bhaer," one
strong brown hand in hers, and a world of affection in his
voice as he said, "I could never forget old friends! How
could I forget the only home I ever knew? Why, I was in
such a hurry to come and tell my good luck that I didn't
stop; though I knew you'd think I looked more like a wild
buffalo than ever."

"I like your look," laughed Mrs. Jo. "You resemble a ban-
dit. Mary, being a newcomer, was frightened at your looks
and manners. Josie won't know you, but Ted will recognize his Danny in spite of the big beard and wild mane.
They will all be here soon to welcome you; so before they
come tell me more about yourself. It's been nearly two
years since you were here, Dan dear. Has it gone well with
you?"

He gave an account of his life in California, and the unexpected success of a small investment he had made. He
explained, "I don't care for the money, you know. I only
want a trifle to pay my way. It's the fun of the thing coming
to me, and my being able to give it away, that I like. No use
to save it up; I shan't live to be old—my sort never do."

"But if you marry and settle somewhere, as I hope you
will, you must have something to begin with, my son. So
be prudent and invest your money; don't give it away, for
rainy days come to all of us."

Dan shook his head, and glanced about the room. "Who would marry a man like me? Women like a steady-going man; I shall never be that."

"My dear boy, when I was a girl I liked just such adventurous fellows as you are. Anything fresh and daring, free and romantic, is always attractive to us women-folk. Don't be discouraged."

"What should you say if I brought you an Indian squaw some day?" asked Dan.

"I would welcome her heartily, if she was a good woman. Is there some chance of it?"

"Not at present. I'm too busy 'to gallivant,' as Ted calls it. How is the boy?" asked Dan, turning the conversation from himself.

Mrs. Jo was off at once, and spoke upon her sons till they came bursting in and fell upon Dan like two affectionate young bears. The professor followed, and all talked up a storm.

After tea Dan was walking up and down the long rooms as he talked, with occasional trips into the hall for a fresh breath of air. In one of those trips he saw a white figure framed in the dark doorway, and paused to look at it. Bess paused also, not at first recognizing her old friend.

"Is it Dan?" she asked, coming in with a smile and an outstretched hand.

"Looks like it; but I didn't know it was you, Princess. I thought it was an angel," answered Dan.

"I've grown very much, but two years have changed you entirely," said Beth.

Before they could say more, Josie rushed in, and let Dan catch her up and kiss her like a child. Not till he set her down did he discover that she also was changed, and exclaimed, "Hello! Why, you are growing up too! What am I going to do, with no young one to play with? Here's Ted growing like a beanstalk, and Bess a young lady, and even you, my mustard-seed, becoming a real lady."

The girls laughed.

Dan shook his head. "Who would marry a man like me?"

"Here!" called Mrs. Jo. "Bring Dan back, and let us keep an eye on him, or he will be slipping off for another year or two."

Led by his pretty captors, Dan returned to the parlor to receive a scolding from little Josie for getting ahead of all the other boys and looking like a man first: "Emil is older; but he's only a boy, and dances jigs and sings sailor songs just as he used to. You look thirty, and as big and dark as a villain in a play. Oh, I've got a splendid idea! You are just the thing for the part of the Egyptian Arbaces in *The Last Days of Pompeii*. We want to act it. You will be gorgeous in red and white shawls. Won't he, Aunt Jo?"

This flood of words made Dan clap his hands over his ears; and before Mrs. Bhaer could answer her niece the Laurences, with Meg and family, arrived, soon followed by Tom and Nan, and all sat down to listen to Dan's adventures. His stories made all the boys want to start at once for California and make their fortunes.

"Of course you will want to go back for another stroke of luck," said Mr. Laurie. "But speculation is a dangerous game, and you may lose all you've won."

"I've had enough of it; it's too much like gambling," explained Dan. "The excitement is all I care for, and it isn't good for me. I have a notion to try farming out West. I feel as if steady work would be good for me."

"That is a capital idea, Dan!" cried Mrs. Jo. "We shall know where you are, and can go and see you, and not have half the world between us. I'll send my Ted for a visit. He's such a restless spirit, it would do him good. With you he would be safe while he worked off his surplus energy and learned a wholesome business."

"I'll use the shovel and the hoe like a good one, if I get a chance out there, but the mines sound rather jollier," said Ted, examining the samples of ore Dan brought for the professor.

"You go and start a new town, and when we are ready to swarm we will come out and settle there. You will want a newspaper very soon, and I like the idea of running one myself much better than grinding away as I do now," observed Demi.

"We could easily plant a new college there," said Mr. March. "Those Westerners are hungry for learning."

"Go on, Dan. It is a fine plan, and we will back you up," said Mr. Laurie, always ready to help the lads to help themselves, both by his cheery words and ever-open wallet.

"I'd like to see what I can do," answered Dan, "though I have my doubts about its suiting me for long. I can cut loose, I suppose, when I'm tired of it."

"I know you won't like it," said Josie. "After having the whole world to roam over, one farm will seem dreadfully small and stupid." She much preferred the romance of the wandering life which brought her thrilling tales and pretty things at each return.

"Is there any art out there?" asked Bess.

"There's plenty of nature, dear," said her father, "and that is much better. You will find splendid animals to sculpt and scenery such as you never saw in Europe to paint."

Bess confessed that studies from nature would be good for her.

"I'll offer to doctor the new town," said Nan. "I shall be ready by the time you get started—towns grow so fast out there."

"Dan isn't going to allow any women under forty in his place," said Tom, very jealous of the admiration Nan showed Dan. "He doesn't like women, especially young and pretty ones."

"That won't affect me," answered Nan, "because doctors are exceptions to all rules. There won't be much sickness in Dansville, everyone will lead such active, wholesome lives, and only energetic young people will go there. But accidents will be frequent, owing to wild cattle, fast riding, Indian fights and the recklessness of Western life. That will just suit me. I long for broken bones, and I find so few here."

"Yes, I'll have you as the doctor," laughed Dan. "I'll send for you as soon as I have a roof to cover you. I'll smash up a dozen cowboys for your special benefit."

"Thanks. I'll come."

But then Dan made haste to unfold another plan seething in that active brain of his: "I'm not sure the farming will succeed, and I have a strong leaning toward my old friends the Montana Indians. They are a peaceful tribe, and need help awfully; hundreds have died of starvation because they don't get their share. The Sioux are fighters, thirty thousand strong, so the government fears 'em, and gives 'em all they want. I call that a shame! If I'd had any money when I was there I'd have given every cent to those poor devils, cheated out of everything, and waiting patiently, after being driven from their own land to places where nothing will grow. Now, honest agents on the reservation could do much for them, and I've a feeling that I ought to go and lend a hand. I know their lingo, and I like 'em. I've got a few thousand dollars, and I ain't sure I have any right to spend it on myself." Dan looked very manly and earnest as he faced his friends, flushed and excited by the energy of his words.

"Do it, do it!" cried Mrs. Jo, fired at once.

"Do it, do it!" echoed Ted, "and take me along to help. I'm just raging to get among those fine fellows and hunt."

"Let us hear more," said Mr. Laurie.

Dan plunged at once into the history of what he saw among the Dakotas and other tribes in the Northwest, telling of their wrongs, patience and courage as if they were his brothers.

"They called me Dan Fire Cloud, because my rifle was the best they ever saw. And Black Hawk was as good a friend as a fellow would want; he saved my life more than once, and taught me just what will be useful if I go back. They are down on their luck, now, and I'd like to pay my debts."

By this time everyone was interested, and the farm town of "Dansville" began to lose its charms. But prudent

Mr. Bhaer suggested that one honest agent among many dishonest ones could not do much, and noble as the effort would be, it was wiser to think over the matter carefully, get influence and authority from the right quarters, and meantime look at some farmland before deciding.

"Well, I will. I'm going to take a run to Kansas and see how that promises. The fact is, there's so much to be done everywhere that I don't know where to go," answered Dan. "I half-wish I didn't have any money."

"I'll keep it for you till you decide," said Mr. Laurie. "You are such an impetuous lad you'll give it to the first beggar that gets hold of you. I'll hand it back when you are ready to invest, shall I?"

"Thanky, sir, I'd be glad to get rid of it. You just hold on till I say the word; and if anything happens to me this time, keep it to help some other scamp as you helped me. This is my will, and you all witness it. Now I feel better."

No one dreamed how much was to happen before Dan came to take his money back.

Meanwhile, a cheery voice was heard singing:

> "Oh, Peggy was a jolly lass,
> Ye heave ho, boys, ye heave ho!"

Emil always announced his arrival in that fashion, and in a moment he came hurrying in with Nat, who had been giving violin lessons in town all day. It was good to see how happy Nat and Dan were to see each other, and it was wonderful, later, to hear Emil and Dan tell stories of their far-flung adventures.

The house could not contain all these young folk, so they migrated to the piazza and settled on the steps, like a flock of birds. Mr. March and the professor retired to the study, while Meg and Amy went to look after the drinks and snacks, and Mrs. Jo and Mr. Laurie sat in the long window listening to the chat that went on outside.

"There they are, the flower of our flock!" she said, pointing to the group of them. "The others are dead or scattered, but these seven boys and four girls are my especial comfort and pride."

"When we remember how different they are, from what some of them came, and the home influences about others, I think we may feel pretty satisfied so far," answered Mr. Laurie, as his eyes rested on his daughter Bess.

"I don't worry about the girls; Meg sees to them, and is so wise and patient and tender they can't help doing well; but my boys are more care every year, and seem to drift farther away from me each time they go," sighed Mrs. Jo. "They will grow up, and I can only hold them by one little thread, which may snap at any time, as it has with Jack and Ned. Dolly and George still like to come back, and I can say my word to them; and dear old Franz is too true ever to forget his own. But the three who are soon going out into the world again I can't help worrying about. Emil's good heart will keep him straight, I hope. And Nat is to make his first flight, but he's weak; and Dan is still untamed. I fear it will take some hard lesson to do that."

"He's a fine fellow, Jo, and I almost regret his farming project. A little polish would make a gentleman of him, and who knows what he might become here among us."

"No, Teddy. Work and the free life he loves will make a good man of him, and that is better than any amount of polish, with the dangers an easy life in the city would bring him. We can't change his nature—only help it to develop in the right direction."

Mrs. Jo spoke earnestly, for, knowing Dan better than anyone else, she saw that her colt was not thoroughly broken yet, and feared while she hoped, knowing that life would always be hard for one like him. She was sure that before he went away again, in some quiet moment he would give her a glimpse of his inner self, and then she could say a word of warning or encouragement that he needed. So she bided her time, studying him meanwhile, glad to see all that was promising, and quick to detect the harm the world was doing him. She was very anxious to make a success of her "firebrand" because others predicted failure; but having learned that people cannot be molded like clay, she contented herself with the hope that this neglected boy might become a good man, and asked no more. Even that was much to expect, so full was he of wayward impulses, strong passions and the lawless nature born in him. Nothing held him but the one affection of his life—the memory of Plumfield, the fear of disappointing these faithful friends, the pride that made him want to keep the regard of the mates who always had admired and loved him in spite of all his faults.

"Don't fret, old dear," said Mr. Laurie. "Emil is one of the happy-go-lucky sorts who always land on their feet. I'll see to Nat, and Dan is in good shape now."

"I hope so.—Now what is that noise?" And Mrs. Jo leaned forward to listen, as exclamations from Teddy and Josie caught her ear.

"A mustang! A real, live one, and we can ride it! Oh, Dan, you are a first-class hero!" cried the boy.

"An Indian dress for me!" added Josie, clapping her hands. "Now I can play the part of Namioka!"

That night, after the young ones had gone to bed, Dan lingered on the piazza, enjoying the warm wind that blew up from the hayfields. And as he leaned there in the moonlight, Mrs. Jo came to shut the door. "Dreaming, Dan?" she asked.

"Not quite—I was wishing I could smoke."

Mrs. Jo laughed, and answered, "You may, in your room; but don't set the house afire."

He stooped and kissed her, saying in a whisper, "Good-night, mother."

Everyone was glad and content the next morning, and all lingered over the breakfast table, till Mrs. Jo suddenly exclaimed, "Why, there's a dog!" And on the threshold of the door appeared a great deerhound standing motionless, with his eyes fixed on Dan.

"Hello, old boy! Couldn't you wait till I came for you?" said Dan, rising to meet the dog, who reared on his hind

legs to look his master in the face. Dan gave Don, the tall
beast, a hug, adding as he glanced out the window, where
a man and a horse were seen approaching, "I left a few of
my surprises at the hotel overnight, not knowing if I was
going to find you all here. Come out now and see Octoo,
my mustang; she's a beauty." And Dan was off, with the
family streaming after him, to welcome the newcomer.

"Well, my girl," he said, as the pretty creature came up
to him and whinnied with pleasure as he rubbed her nose
and patted her glossy flank, "do you want to gallop?"

"That's what I call a horse worth having," said Ted, full
of admiration and delight; for he was to have the care of
her during Dan's absence.

"What does 'Octoo' mean?" asked Rob.

"'Lightning.' She deserves the name, as you'll see. The
great Black Hawk gave her to me for my rifle, and we've
had high times together out yonder. She's saved my life
more than once. Do you see that scar of hers?" Dan
pointed to a small one, half hidden by her long mane; and
standing with his arm about Octoo's neck, he told the
story of it.

"Black Hawk and I were after buffalo one time, but
didn't find 'em as soon as we expected; so our food gave
out, and there we were a hundred miles from Red Deer
River, where our camp was. I thought we were done for,
but my brave pal says, 'Now I'll show you how we can live
till we find the herds.' We were unsaddling for the night by
a little pond; there wasn't a living creature in sight anywhere, not even a bird, and we could see for miles over
the prairies. What do you think we did?" And Dan looked
into the faces around him.

"Ate worms?" said Rob.

"Boiled grass or leaves?" said Mrs. Jo.

"Perhaps filled the stomach with clay, as we read of Indians doing?" suggested Mr. Bhaer.

"Killed one of the horses!" cried Ted.

"No; but we bled one of them. See, just here, we filled a
tin cup of Octoo's blood, put some wild sage leaves in it,

with water, and heated it over a fire of sticks. It was good,
and we slept well."

"I guess Octoo didn't," said Josie, patting the animal.

"Never minded it a bit. Black Hawk said we could live on
the horses several days and still travel before they felt it.
But by that next morning we found the buffalo, and I shot
the one whose head is in my box. He was a fierce old
fellow."

"What is this strap for?" asked Ted, who was busily examining the Indian saddle, the single rein and snaffle, with
lariat, and round the neck the leather band he spoke of.

"We hold on to that when we lie along the horse's flank
farthest from the enemy, and fire under the neck as we
gallop round and round. I'll show you." And springing into
the saddle, Dan was off down the steps, tearing over the
lawn at a great pace, sometimes on Octoo's back, sometimes half hidden as he hung by stirrup and strap, and
sometimes off altogether, running beside her as she loped
along, enjoying the fun immensely; while Don the dog
raced after, in joy at being free again and with his friends.

"That is better than a circus!" cried Mrs. Jo, wishing she
were a girl again, that she might take a gallop on this
chained lightning of a horse. "I foresee that Nan will have
her hands full setting bones, for Ted will break every one
of his trying to rival Dan."

"A few falls will not harm, and this caring for the horse
will be good for Ted in all ways. But I fear Dan will never
follow a plow on a farmer's slow horse after riding a Pe-
gasus like that," answered Mr. Bhaer, as the black mare
leaped the gate and came flying up the avenue, to stop at
a word and stand quivering with excitement, while Dan
swung himself off and looked up for applause.

He received plenty of it. Ted clamored for a lesson at
once, and was soon at ease in the saddle, finding Octoo
gentle as a lamb, as he trotted away to show off at college.

It was interesting to see what a pleasant stir Dan's and
Emil's coming made in the quiet life of the college; for they
seemed to bring a fresh breeze with them that enlivened

everyone. Many of the college students remained during vacation; and Plumfield and Parnassus did their best to make these days pleasant for them, since most came from distant States, were poor and had few opportunities but this for culture or amusement. Emil was at ease with men and maids, and went rollicking about in true sailor fashion; but Dan stood rather in awe of the "fair girl-graduates," and was silent when among them, eyeing them as an eagle might a flock of doves. He got on better with the young men, and was their hero at once. Their admiration for his manly accomplishments did him good; because he felt his educational defects keenly, and often wondered if he could find anything in books to satisfy him as thoroughly as did the lessons he was learning from Nature. In spite of his shyness, the girls found out his good qualities, and regarded him with great favor.

After the life in California, it was sweet and restful to be here, with these familiar faces round him. There was riding, rowing and picnicking by day, music, dancing and plays by night; and everyone said there had not been so merry a vacation for years.

Meanwhile, Nat was snatching every minute he could get with Daisy before the long parting; and Mrs. Meg allowed this, somewhat, feeling sure that absence would quite cure this unfortunate budding love. Daisy said little, but her gentle face was sad when she was alone. She was sure Nat would not forget her; and her life ahead looked rather empty without the dear fellow who had been her friend since the playful childhood days. But she kept her little sorrow to herself, and made Nat's last days of home-life very happy with sweet words and thoughtful going-away gifts.

A few weeks were all they had; then the *Brenda* was ready, Nat was to sail from New York, and Dan went along to see him off; for his own plans were baking in his head, and he was eager to be up and about. A farewell dance was given on Parnassus in honor of the travellers, and all turned out in the best clothes and merriest spirits.

Emil was glorious in his new uniform, and danced with an abandon which only sailors knew. His shoes seemed to be everywhere at once, and his partners soon lost breath trying to keep up with him; but the girls all declared he danced like an angel, so he was happy.

Having no dress clothes, Dan had been persuaded to wear his Mexican costume, and feeling at ease in the many-buttoned trousers, loose jacket and bright sash, flung his *serape* over his shoulder and looked his best, as he taught Josie strange steps.

Amy, Jo and Meg sat in the alcove, supplying smiles and kindly words to all.

During supper, there was lively group eating on the stairs, girls at the top, and young men below. Emil, who never sat if he could perch, was upon the post; Tom, Nat, Demi and Dan were camped on the steps, eating busily, as their ladies were well served, and they had earned a moment's rest.

"I'm so sorry the boys are going. It will be dreadfully dull without them. Now that they have stopped teasing and are polite, I really enjoy them," said Nan.

"So do I," said Daisy. "And Bess was mourning about it today. She has been sculpting Dan's head, and it is not quite finished. I never saw her so interested in any work, and it's very well done. He is so striking and big. There's Bess now. Dear child, how sweet she looks tonight."

And Bess went by with Grandpa on her arm.

"I never thought Dan would turn out so well," said Nan. "Don't you remember how we used to call him 'the bad boy,' and be sure he would become a pirate or something awful because he glared at us and swore sometimes? Now he is the handsomest of all the boys, and very entertaining with his stories and plans. I like him very much; he's so big and strong and independent. I'm tired of mamma's boys and bookworms."

"Not handsomer than Nat!" cried loyal Daisy. "I like Dan, and am glad he is doing well. But he tires me, and I'm still a little afraid of him. Quiet people suit me best."

Nan objected: "Life is a fight, and I like a good warrior. Boys take things too easily, don't see how serious it all is. Look at that silly Tom, wasting his time and making an object of himself just because he can't have what he wants, like a baby crying for the moon. I've no patience with such nonsense."

"Most girls would be touched by such love. I think it's beautiful," said Daisy.

"You are a sentimental goose and not a judge. Nat will be twice the man when he comes back after his trip. I wish Tom was going with him. My idea is that if we girls have any influence we should use it for the good of these boys, and not pamper them, making slaves of ourselves and tyrants of them. Let them prove what they can do and be before they ask anything of us, and give us a chance to do the same. Then we know where we are, and shall not make mistakes to mourn over all our lives."

"Hear, hear!" cried Alice Heath, Nan's friend, who was a girl after Nan's own heart, and had chosen a career, like a brave and sensible young woman. "Only give us a chance, and have patience till we can do our best. Now we are expected to be as wise as men who have had generations of all the help there is, and we scarcely anything. Let us have equal opportunities, and in a few generations we will see what the judgment is. I like justice, and we get very little of it."

The boys were listening now, and all began laughing and talking at once. Bess then came floating through the upper hall and looked down like an angel of peace upon the noisy group below. She asked, with wondering eyes and smiling lips, "What is it?"

"Nan and Alice are on a rampage, and accusing us of crimes," answered Demi. "Will your highness judge between us?"

"I'm not wise enough," answered Bess. "I'll sit here and listen. Please go on." And Bess took her place above them all as cool and calm as a little statue of Justice.

"Now, ladies, speak your minds, only quickly," said

Demi, "as we've got a dance to dance as soon as everyone is fed."

"I have only one thing to say, and it is this," began Nan. "I want to ask every boy of you what you really think on this subject. Dan and Emil have seen the world and ought to know their own minds. Tom and Nat have had fine examples before them for years. Demi is ours and we are proud of him. So is Rob. Ted goes any way the wind blows, and Dolly and George of course are old fogies, in spite of girl students being far ahead of them. Commodore Emil, are you ready for the question?"

"Ay, ay, skipper."

"Do you believe in the right of women to vote?"

"Bless your pretty head! I do, and I'll sail a ship of girls any time you say so. Don't we all need one as pilot to steer us safe to port? And why shouldn't they share our life afloat and ashore since we are sure to be wrecked without 'em?"

"Good for you, Emil! Nan will take you for first mate after that speech," said Demi, as the girls applauded.

"Now, Dan, you love liberty so well yourself, are you willing we should have the vote?"

"All you can get, and I'll fight any man who's mean enough to say you don't deserve it."

This brief reply delighted Nan, and she beamed as she said, "Nat wouldn't dare say he was on the other side, even if he were, but I hope he has made up his mind to pipe for us, at least when we take the field, and not be one of those who wait till the battle is won."

Nat answered, "I should be the most ungrateful fellow alive if I did not love, honor and serve women with all my heart and might, for to them I owe everything I am or ever shall be."

Daisy clapped her hands, and Bess tossed her bouquet into Nat's lap, while the other girls waved their fans.

"Thomas B. Bangs, come into the court of women and tell the truth, the whole truth and nothing but the truth, if you can," commanded Nan.

Daisy clapped her hands, and Bess tossed her bouquet into Nat's lap.

Tom stood up and raised his hand, saying, "I believe in women's rights. I adore all women, and will die for them at any moment if it will help the cause."

"Living and working for our rights is harder, and therefore more honorable. Men are always ready to die for us, but not to make our lives worth having. You will pass, Tom, only don't speak twaddle. I am glad to see that old Plum has given six true men to the world, and hope they will continue to support the causes of women. Now, let us call an end to this meeting and go on to the dance."

4. Last Words

The next day was Sunday, and a large troop of young and old set forth to church—some in carriages, some walking, all enjoying the lovely weather and the happy peacefulness that comes to refresh us when the work and worry of the week are over. Daisy had a headache; and Aunt Jo remained at home to keep her company, knowing very well that the worst ache was in the girl's tender heart.

"Daisy knows my wishes," Mrs. Meg told her sister while waiting for Demi to escort her to church, "and I trust her not to disobey me. You must keep an eye on Nat, however, and let him clearly understand that there is to be no lovey-doveying, or I shall forbid them writing letters to each other. I hate to seem cruel, but it is too soon for my dear girl to become engaged."

"I will keep my eye on him, dear," answered Jo. "I'm lying in wait for three boys today, like an old spider; and I will have a good talk with each. They know I understand them, and they always open their hearts sooner or later."

"Be firm with Nat, Jo, and don't give in."

Then, having buttoned her gloves with care, Meg took her son's arm and went proudly away to the carriage, where Amy and Bess waited, while Jo called after them, just as Marmee used to do, "Girls, have you got nice pocket-handkerchiefs?" They all smiled at the familiar words, and three white hankies waved as they drove away, leaving Jo the spider to watch for her first fly. She did not wait long.

Dan had gone for a ten-mile stroll; and Nat was sup-
posed to have accompanied him, but soon came sneaking
back, unable to tear himself away from the home of his
darling. Mrs. Jo saw him at once, and beckoned him to a
seat under the old elm, where they could have their talk,
and both keep an eye on the window which contained
Daisy.

"Nice and cool here," said Nat, fanning himself with his
straw hat. "I'm not up to one of Dan's tramps today—it's
so warm, and he goes so like a steam-engine. He headed
for the swamp where his pet snakes used to live, and I
begged to be excused."

"I'm glad you did. Sit and rest with me, and have one of
our good old talks. We've both been so busy lately, I feel
as if I didn't half know your plans; and I want to."

"You are very kind, and there's nothing I'd like better. I
don't realize I'm going so far away—and suppose I won't
till I get on the boat. It's a splendid chance for me, and I
don't know how I can ever thank Mr. Laurie for all he's
done, or you either," added Nat.

"You can thank us beautifully by being and doing all we
hope and expect of you, my dear. In the new life you are
going to there will be a thousand trials and temptations,
and only your own wit and wisdom to rely on. That will be
the time to test the principles we have tried to give you,
and see how firm they are. Of course you will make mistakes—we all do; but don't let go of your conscience and
drift along blindly. Watch and pray, Nat; and while you
gain skill on the violin, learn from your life, and keep your
heart as innocent and warm as it is now."

"I'll try my very best to be a credit to you, Mother
Bhaer. I know I shall improve in my music—can't help it
there; but I never shall be very wise, I'm afraid. As for my
heart, you know I leave it here."

As he spoke, Nat's eyes were fixed on the window with
a look of love.

Jo said, "I want to speak of just that; and I know you will
forgive what seems hard, because I do feel for you."

"Yes, do talk about Daisy! I think of nothing but leaving and losing her. I have no hope—I suppose it is too much to ask; only I can't help loving her, wherever I am!" cried Nat.

"Listen to me and I'll try to give you both comfort and good advice. We all know that Daisy is fond of you, but her mother objects, and being a good girl she tries to obey. Young people think they never can change, but they do in the most wonderful manner, and very few die of broken hearts." Mrs. Jo smiled as she remembered Laurie, another boy whom she had once tried to comfort, and then went on while Nat listened. "One of two things will happen. You will find someone else to love, or, better still, be so busy and happy in your music that you will be willing to wait for time to settle the matter for you both. Daisy will perhaps forget when you are gone, and be glad you are only friends. At any rate it is much wiser to have no promises made; then both are free, and in a year or two you may meet to laugh over the little romance nipped in the bud."

"Do you honestly think that?" asked Nat.

"No, I don't!" answered Jo.

"Then if you were in my place, what would you do?"

"Bless me!" thought Mrs. Jo, "the boy is as serious about this as could be. I shall forget to be wise." She was surprised and pleased by the manliness Nat showed. "I'll tell you what I should do. I'd say to myself, 'I'll prove that my love is strong and faithful, and make Daisy's mother proud to give her to me by being not only a good musician but an excellent man, and so command respect and confidence. This I will try for; and if I fail, I shall be the better for the effort, and find comfort in the thought that I did my best for her sake.'"

"That is what I meant to do. But I wanted a word of hope to give me courage," cried Nat. "Other fellows, poorer and stupider than I, have done great things and come to honor. Why may not I, though I'm nothing now? I know

Mrs. Brooke remembers what I came from, but my father was honest though everything went wrong; and I have nothing to be ashamed of though I was a charity boy. I never will be ashamed of my people or myself, and I'll make other folks respect me if I can."

"Good! that's the right spirit, Nat. Hold to it and make yourself a man. No one will be quicker to see and admire the brave work than my sister Meg. She does not despise your poverty or your past; but mothers are very tender over their daughters, and we Marches, though we have been poor, *are*, I confess, a little proud of our good family. We don't care for money; but a long line of good ancestors is something to desire and to be proud of."

"Well, we Blakes are a good lot. I looked 'em up, and not one was ever in prison, hanged or disgraced in any way. My father was a street musician rather than beg; and I'll be one before I'll do the bad things some men do."

"I am sure if you do well these next few years that she will relent and all be happily settled, unless the amazing change of heart, which you don't believe possible, should occur. Now, cheer up; don't be blue. Say goodbye cheerfully and bravely, show a manly front, and leave a pleasant memory behind you. We all wish you well and hope much for you. Surprise us by your success. Be careful what you write to Daisy; don't gush or cry, for sister Meg will see the letters; and you can help your cause very much by sending sensible, cheery accounts of your life to us all."

"I will; I will; it looks brighter and better already. Thank you so much, Mother Bhaer, for taking my side."

"Remember, Nat, it is that struggle with obstacles which does us good. Things have been made easy for you in many ways, but no one can do everything. You must paddle your own canoe now. I only hope you won't work too hard."

"I'll take care."

Just then they saw Emil strolling on the roof of the old house, that being his favorite spot now; for up there he could fancy himself walking the deck, with only blue sky and fresh air about him.

"I want a word with the Commodore, and up there we shall be nice and quiet. Go and play your violin for Daisy; it will put her to sleep and do you both good. Sit on the porch, though, so I can keep an eye on you as I promised Mrs. Meg." And with a motherly pat on the shoulder, Mrs. Jo left Nat to his delightful task and went inside up the stairs to the housetop.

As she emerged on the roof, Emil said, "Come aboard and make yourself at home, Aunty."

Mrs. Jo took a seat near where he sat astride the balustrade. She began, "I often wish I could sail away, and some day I will, when you are captain, and have a ship of your own."

"When I do have one, I'll christen her the *Jolly Jo,* and take you as first mate. It would be fun to have you aboard, and I'd be a proud man to carry you round the world you've wanted to see so long and never could."

"I'll make my first voyage with you and enjoy myself immensely in spite of the seasickness and all the storms. But this new voyage you're about to take will give you new duties. Are you ready for them? You take everything so lightly, I've been wondering if you realized that now you will have not only to obey but to command also, and power is a dangerous thing. Be careful that you don't abuse it or let it make a tyrant of you. And don't get into trouble, for even your uncle Hermann's help won't cover that. You have proved yourself a good sailor; now be a good officer, which is a harder thing, I fancy. It takes a good character to rule justly and kindly."

"Right you are, ma'am. I'll do my best. I know my time for fooling is over, and I must steer a straighter course. I had a long talk with Uncle Fritz last night and he steered me right as well." And Emil gave his aunt a hearty kiss.

"You do me proud, Captain. But, dear, I want to say one thing and then I'm done; for you don't need much advice of mine after my good husband has spoken. I read somewhere that every inch of rope used in the British Navy has a strand of red in it, so that wherever a bit of it is found it is known. That is the text of my little sermon to you. Virtue is the red thread that marks a good man wherever he is. Keep that red thread always and everywhere, so that even if wrecked by misfortune, that red thread shall still be found."

As she spoke Emil had risen and stood listening with his cap off, and when she ended, he answered, "Please God, I will!"

"That's all; I have little fear for you, but one never knows when or how a chance word may help us."

"Often in my watch on the deck I've almost sworn I could hear your voice in my ear, aunty. But don't worry about me, and I'll come home next year. Going below now? I'll be along by the time the cake is served. This is my last chance for a good meal ashore."

Mrs. Jo went down the stairs laughing, and Emil continued pacing, whistling cheerfully, neither of them dreaming of the day when this little chat on the housetop would return to his memory.

Dan was harder to catch, and not until evening did a quiet moment come in that busy family; then, while the rest were roaming about, Mrs. Jo sat down to read in the study, and soon Dan looked in at the window.

"Come and rest after your long tramp; you must be tired," she called.

"Afraid I shall disturb you," said Dan.

"Not a bit; I'm always ready to talk, shouldn't be a woman if I were not," laughed Mrs. Jo, as Dan swung himself in and sat down.

"My last day has come," he said, "yet somehow I don't seem to hanker to be off. Generally, I'm rather anxious to cut loose after a short stop. Odd, ain't it?"

"Not at all; you are beginning to get civilized. It's a good sign, and I'm glad to see it. You've had your adventures, and want a change. I hope the farming will give it to you, though helping the Indians pleases me more—it is so much better to work for others than for one's self alone."

"So it is," agreed Dan. "I seem to want to put down roots somewhere and have folks of my own to take care of. Tired of my own company, I suppose. I'm a rough sort, and I've been thinking maybe I've missed something by not going in for education as the other chaps did."

"No," said Mrs. Jo, "I don't think so in your case. So far I'm sure the free life was best. Now that you are a man you can control that lawless nature better; but as a boy only great activity and much adventure could keep you out of mischief. Time is taming my colt, you see, and I shall yet be proud of him."

Dan smiled. "Glad you think so. The fact is it's going to take a heap of taming to make me go well. I want to, and I try now and then, but always end up running off. No lives lost yet; but I shouldn't be surprised if there was some time."

"Why, Dan, did you have any dangerous adventures during this last absence? I fancied so, but didn't ask before, knowing you'd tell me if I could help in any way. Can I?"

"Nothing very bad; but Frisco isn't any heaven on earth, you know, and it's harder to be a saint there than here," he answered. "I tried gambling, and it wasn't good for me."

"Was that how you made your money?"

"Not a penny of it! But I don't know if speculation isn't a bigger sort of gambling. Anyway, I won a lot gambling; but I threw it all away and stopped before the game got the better of me."

"Thank heaven for that! Don't try it again; it may have the terrible fascination for you it has for so many. Keep to your mountains and prairies, and shun cities, if these things tempt you, Dan. Better lose your life than your soul, and one such passion leads to worse sins, as you know better than I."

Dan nodded, and seeing how troubled she was, said, in a lighter tone, "Don't be scared; I'm all right now; and a burnt dog dreads the fire. I don't drink, or do the things you dread; I don't care for 'em; but I get excited, and then this devilish temper of mine is more than I can manage. Fighting a moose or a buffalo is all right; but when you pitch into a man, no matter how great a scamp he is, you've got to look out. I shall kill someone some day; that's all I'm afraid of. I do hate a sneak!" And Dan brought his fist down on the table with a blow that made the lamp totter and the books hop.

"That always was your trial, Dan, and I can sympathize with you; for I've been trying to govern my own temper all my life, and haven't learnt yet," said Mrs. Jo, with a sigh. "For heaven's sake, guard your demon well, and don't let a moment's fury ruin all your life. As I said to Nat, watch and pray, my dear boy. There is no other help or hope for human weakness but God's love and patience."

Tears were in Mrs. Jo's eyes as she spoke; for she felt this deeply, and knew how hard a task it is to rule these deep faults of ours. Dan looked touched, also uncomfortable, as he always did when religion of any sort was mentioned.

"I don't do much praying; don't seem to come handy to me; but I can watch like an Indian, only it's easier to mount guard over a lurking grizzly bear than my own cursed temper. It's that I'm afraid of, if I settle down. I can get on with wild beasts first-rate; but men rile me awfully, and I can't take it out in a free fight, as I can with a bear or a wolf. Guess I'd better head for the Rockies, and stay there a spell longer—till I'm tame enough for decent folks, if I ever am."

"Try my sort of help, and don't give up. Read more, study a little and try to meet a better class of people, who won't rile you, but soothe and strengthen you. We don't make you savage, I'm sure; for you have been as meek as a lamb, and made us very happy."

"Glad of it; but I've felt like a hawk in a henhouse all the same, and wanted to pounce more than once. Not so much as I used to, though," added Dan. "I'll try your plan, and keep good company if I can; but a man can't pick and choose, knocking about as I do."

"Yes, you can this time; for you are going on a peaceful errand and can keep clear of temptation if you try. Take some books and read; that's an immense help; and books are always good company if you have the right sort. Let me pick out some for you." And Mrs. Jo made a bee-line to the bookshelves, which were the joy of her heart and comfort of her life.

"Give me travels and stories, please; don't want any pious works, can't seem to relish 'em, and won't pretend I do," said Dan.

"Now, Dan, see here; never sneer at good things or pretend to be worse than you are. You needn't talk of religion if you don't like, but don't shut your heart to it in whatever shape it comes. Nature is your God now; she has done much for you; let her do more, and lead you to know and love a wiser and more tender teacher, friend and comforter than she can ever be. That is your only hope; don't throw it away, and waste time; for sooner or later you'll feel the need of Him, and He will come to you and hold you up when all other help fails."

Dan did not speak, but his eyes softened.

Mrs. Jo went on, with her most motherly smile, "I saw in your room the little Bible I gave you long ago; it was well worn outside, but fresh within, as if not much read. Will you promise me to read a little once a week, dear, for my sake? Sunday is a quiet day everywhere, and this book is never old nor out of place. Begin with the stories you used to love when I told them to you boys. David was your favorite, you remember? Read about him again; he'll suit you even better now, and you'll find his sins and repentance useful reading till you come to the life and work of a diviner example than he. You will do it, for love of Mother Bhaer, who always loved her firebrand and hoped to save him?"

"I will," answered Dan.

Mrs. Jo turned at once to the books and began to talk of them, knowing well that Dan would not bear any more soul-searching just then. He seemed relieved; for it was always hard for him to show his inner self, and he took pride in hiding it.

He opened one of the books and exclaimed, "Hello! Here's old Sintram! I remember him; used to like him and his tantrums, and read about 'em to Ted. There he is riding ahead with Death and the Devil alongside."

As Dan looked at the little picture of the young man with horse and hound going bravely up the rocky cliff, accompanied by companions who represented danger, Mrs. Jo said, "That's you, Dan, just you at this time! Danger and sin are near you in the life you lead; moods and passions torment you; the bad father left you to fight alone, and the wild spirit drives you to wander up and down the world looking for peace and self-control. Even the horse and hound are there, your Octoo and Don, faithful friends, unscared by the strange mates that go with you. You have not got Christ's armor yet, but I'm trying to show you where to find it. You remember the mother Sintram loved and longed to find, and did find when his battle was bravely fought, his reward well earned? You can recollect your mother; and I have always felt that all the good qualities you possess come from her. Act out the beautiful old story in this as in the other parts, and try to give her back a son to be proud of."

The story of poor, tormented Sintram came back clearly as he looked and listened, symbolizing his secret trials even more truly than Mrs. Jo knew; and just at that moment this had an effect upon him that never was forgotten. But all he said was, "Small chance of that. I don't take much stock in the idea of meeting folks in heaven. I guess Mother won't remember the poor little brat she left so long ago; why should she?"

"Because true mothers never forget their children; and I know she was one, from the fact that she ran away from the cruel husband to save her little son from bad influences. Had she lived, life would have been happier for you with this tender friend to help and comfort you. Never forget that she risked everything for your sake, and don't let it be in vain."

Mrs. Jo spoke very earnestly, knowing that this was the one sweet memory of Dan's early life; but suddenly a great tear splashed down on the page where Sintram kneels at his mother's feet, wounded, but victorious over sin and death. Jo looked up, well pleased to have touched Dan to the heart's core, as that teardrop proved; but a sweep of the arm brushed away the tear, and his beard hid another, as he shut the book, saying, "I'll keep this book, if nobody wants it. I'll read it over, and maybe it will do me good. I'd like to meet her anywhere, but don't believe I ever shall."

"Keep it and welcome. My mother gave it to me; and when you read it try to believe that neither of your mothers will ever forget you."

"Thanks," said Dan. "Good night." He thrust the book into his pocket, and walked straight away to the river to recover from this tender moment.

The next day the travellers were off. All were in good spirits, and a cloud of handkerchiefs whitened the air as they drove away, waving their hats to everyone and kissing their hands, especially to Mother Bhaer, who said as she wiped her eyes, "I have a feeling that something is going to happen to some of them, and they will never come back to me, or will come back changed. Well, I can only say, 'God be with my boys!'"

And He was.

5. The Actress

When the boys were gone a lull fell upon Plumfield, and the family scattered to various places for brief outings, as August had come and all felt the need of change. The professor took Mrs. Jo to the mountains. The Laurences were at the seashore, and there Meg's family and the Bhaer boys took turns to visit, as someone must always be at home to keep things in order.

While the young Bhaer boys were home, Josie was enjoying herself immensely at Rocky Nook; for the Laurences knew how to make summer idleness both charming and wholesome. Bess was very fond of her little cousin Josie, while Mrs. Amy felt that whether her niece was an actress or not she must be a gentlewoman, and gave her the social training which marks the well-bred woman everywhere. Uncle Laurie was never happier than when rowing, riding, playing or lounging with the two cheerful girls beside him. Josie bloomed like a wild flower in this free life, and Bess grew rosy and lively; both were favorites with the neighbors, whose villas were by the shore or perched on the cliffs along the pretty bay.

One disappointed wish, however, disturbed Josie's peace, and kept her as restless as a detective on the case. Miss Cameron, a great actress, had rented one of the villas for the summer and had gone there to rest for a new part the next season. She had no visitors but a friend or two, had a private beach and was never seen except

during her daily drive. The Laurences knew her, but re-
spected her privacy and after a call left her in peace.

But Josie was like a thirsty fly buzzing about a sealed
honey-pot, for this nearness to her idol was both delightful and maddening. She pined to see, hear, talk with and
study this great and happy woman who could thrill thou-
sands by her acting. This was the sort of actress the girl
meant to be. If kindly Miss Cameron had known what pas-
sionate love and longing burned in the bosom of the girl
whom she had idly observed skipping over the rocks,
splashing about the beach or galloping past her gate on a
pony, she would have made her happy by a look or a
word. But being tired with her year's work and busy with
her new part, the lady took no more notice of this young
neighbor than of the seagulls in the bay or the daisies
dancing in the fields. Bouquets left on her doorstep, night
songs under her garden wall and the stares of admiring
eyes were such familiar things that she scarcely minded
them; and Josie grew desperate to meet her.

"I might climb the pine tree and tumble off on her piazza roof, or get Jervey (the pony) to throw me just at her
gate and be taken in fainting. It's no use to try to drown
myself when she is swimming. I can't sink, and she'd only
send a servant to pull me out. What can I do? I will see her
and tell her my hopes and make her say I might well be a
successful actress some day. Mamma would believe her;
and if—oh, if she only would let me study with her, what
perfect joy that would be!"

Josie made these remarks one afternoon as she and
Bess prepared for a swim.

"You must bide your time, dear, and not be so impa-
tient. Papa promised to give you a chance before the summer is over, and he always manages things nicely. That
will be better than any prank of yours," answered Bess.

"I hate to wait; but I suppose I must. Come and have a
good dive from the big rock."

Away they went to have a fine time; for the little bay
was free from other swimmers. As they sat dripping on

the big rock, Josie suddenly gave a start, and said, "There she is! Look! Coming down to swim. How splendid! Oh, if she only would start to drown and let me save her! Or even get her toe nipped by a crab; anything so I could go and speak to her."

"Don't seem to look, Josie! She comes to have peace and enjoy herself. Pretend we don't see her—that would be better," answered Bess.

"No, let's carelessly float that way, as if going after the seaweed on the rocks."

Just as they were about to slip from their rock, by a stroke of kind fate, Miss Cameron beckoned to them, as she stood waist-deep in the water, looking down.

"She wants us! She wants us!" cried Josie, tumbling into the water, and swimming away in her best style. Bess followed more slowly, and both came panting and smiling up to Miss Cameron, who never lifted her eyes, but said in her wonderful voice:

"I've dropped a bracelet. I see it, but can't get it. Will you, the boy, find me a long stick? I'll keep my eye on it, so the water shall not wash it away."

"I'll dive for it with pleasure; but I'm not a boy," answered Josie, laughing as she shook her curly head.

"I beg your pardon, darling," said Miss Cameron. "But dive away; the sand is covering it fast. I value it very much, and never forgot to take it off before."

"I'll get it!" and down went Josie. She came up, moments later, with a handful of pebbles, but no bracelet.

"It's gone!" said Miss Cameron. "But never mind—it's my fault."

"It's not gone," said Josie. "I'll get it, if I have to dive down all day." And with one long breath Josie dived again, leaving nothing but her feet wagging above the surf.

"I'm afraid she'll hurt herself," said Miss Cameron looking at the girl she thought she recognized.

"Oh, no. Josie is a little fish," remarked Bess.

"You are Mr. Laurence's daughter, I think? How do you do, my dear? Tell your papa I'm coming to visit soon. Been

"I'll get it yet," panted Josie, and down she went again.

too tired, you know, but I'm better now. Ah, here's our pearl-diver!"

"Never give up, that's my motto. I'll get it yet," panted Josie. "Now then!" and down she went again.

"Who's the plucky little girl?" asked the lady.

Bess told her, adding, "Josie longs to be an actress, and has waited for a month to see you. This is a great happiness for her."

"Bless the child! But why didn't she come and call? I'd have let her in."

Just then a slim hand, grasping the bracelet, rose out of the sea, followed by Josie, triumphant.

"Bravo, bravo!" laughed Miss Cameron.

Never in Josie's wildest dreams had she imagined a meeting like this.

"Now, my dear," said Miss Cameron, "try to get your breath. It was very nice of you to take all that trouble for me. How shall I thank you?"

"Let me come and see you once! I want you to tell me if I can act; you will know. I'll go by what you say; and if you think I can—by and by, when I've studied very hard—I shall be the happiest girl in the world. May I?"

"Yes; come tomorrow at eleven. We'll have a good talk; you shall show me what you can do, and I'll give you my opinion. But you might not like it!"

"I will so, no matter if you tell me I'm the worst. I want it settled; so does mamma. I'll take it bravely if you say I should give up; but if you say I shouldn't, I'll never stop working till I've done my best—as you did."

"Ah, my child, it's a long, weary road, and there are plenty of thorns among the roses when you've won them. In any case, come tomorrow and we'll see."

"We are keeping Miss Cameron from her swim, and the tide is going out. Let's go, Josie," said thoughtful Bess, fearing to outstay their welcome.

"Thank you very much, little mermaid," said Miss Cameron. "Till tomorrow! Good bye!" And with a wave of her hand the queen of tragedy slipped away into the water.

Of course Josie never slept a wink that night, and was in a fever of joyful excitement the next day. Uncle Laurie enjoyed the story of the meeting very much, and Aunt Amy was pleased her niece had reason to make an early visit to the actress. In the morning Josie ranged the wood and marsh for a bouquet of wild roses, sweet azalea, ferns and graceful grasses, as the offering of a very grateful heart.

"Oh, Bess, pray that she will tell me something good! So much depends on that. Don't laugh, Uncle! It is a very serious moment for me. Miss Cameron knows that, and she will tell you so. Kiss me, Aunt Amy, since Mamma isn't here. If you say I look nice, I'm quite satisfied. Goodbye." And with a wave of the hand as much like Miss Cameron's as she could make it, Josie departed, looking very pretty.

She rang at Miss Cameron's door, and was ushered by a butler into a shady parlor. After a few moments, Miss Cameron swept into the room, and after a few words of greeting, plunged into the middle of things, well knowing that no common chat would satisfy this very earnest little person. "Show me what you can do."

"First let me give you these. I thought you'd like wild things better than hothouse flowers," said Josie, offering the bouquet.

"I do love them best, and keep my room full of the posies some good fairy hangs on my gate."

"I couldn't help it," laughed Josie. "I couldn't get in myself, so I loved to think my flowers pleased you."

"They did please me, dear, and so do you.—Come, now, and show me what you can do. You'll begin with Juliet, I'm sure. They all do." She sounded weary.

Now Josie had intended to begin with Romeo's sweetheart, and follow her up with Bianca, Pauline and several of the favorite idols of stage-struck girls; but being a shrewd girl, she changed her plans. So instead of the rant Miss Cameron expected, Josie gave poor Ophelia's mad scene, and gave it very well. She was too young, of course;

but her white gown, loose hair, and the real flowers she scattered over an imaginary grave as she spoke the words surprised her audience. Miss Cameron applauded, and Josie followed with acting a lively simple girl, telling a story full of fun and naughtiness at first, but ending with a sob of repentance and an earnest prayer for pardon.

"Very good! Try another. Better than I expected," called Miss Cameron.

Josie tried Portia's speech, and recited it very well; then, unable to pass up Juliet, burst into the balcony scene. She felt sure she had surpassed herself, and waited for Miss Cameron to clap. Instead, the famous actress laughed.

In a tone of polite surprise, Josie said, "I have been told that I do that very well. I'm sorry you don't think so."

"My dear, it's very bad. How can it help being so? What can a child like you know of love and fear and death? Don't try it yet. Leave tragedy alone till you are ready for it."

"But you liked Ophelia!"

"Yes, that was very pretty. But any clever girl can do that. The real meaning of Shakespeare is above you yet, child. The comedy bit was best. There you showed real talent. It was both comic and pathetic. That's art. Don't lose it. The Portia was good declamation. Go on with that sort of thing; it's good training and teaches shades of expression. You've a good voice and natural grace—great helps both, hard to acquire."

"Well, I'm glad I've got something," sighed Josie.

"My dear little girl, I told you that you would not like what I should say to you; yet I must be honest, if I would really help you. I've had to do it for many like you; and most of them have never forgiven me, though my words have proved true, and they are what I advised them to be—good wives and happy mothers in quiet homes. Geniuses are very rare."

"Oh, I don't think I'm a genius!" cried Josie. "I only want

to find out if I have talent enough to go on, and after years of study be able to act well in any of the good plays people never tire of seeing. I don't expect to be as good as you, but it does seem as if I had something in me which can't come out in any way but this. When I act I'm perfectly happy. I seem to live, to be in my own world, and each new part is a new friend. I love Shakespeare, and am never tired of his splendid people. Of course I don't understand it all; but it's like being alone at night with the mountains and the stars, solemn and grand, and I try to imagine how it will look when the sun comes up, and all is glorious and clear to me. I can't see, but I feel the beauty, and long to express it."

As she spoke, Josie was pale with excitement, her eyes shone, her lips trembled, and all her little soul seemed trying to put into words the emotions that filled it to overflowing. Miss Cameron understood, and when she answered there was a new tone of sympathy in her voice, a new interest in her face.

"If you feel this, I can give you no better advice than to go on loving and studying our great master," she said slowly. "It is an education in itself, and a lifetime is not long enough to teach you all his secrets. But there is much to do before you can hope to echo his words. Have you the patience, courage and strength to begin at the beginning, and slowly, painfully lay the foundation for future work? Fame is a pearl many dive for and only a few bring up. Even when they do, it is not perfect, and they sigh for more, and lose better things in struggling for them."

Josie answered quickly, with a smile, "I got the bracelet in spite of all the saltwater in my eyes."

"You did! I don't forget it. It's a good omen." Then, in a different tone, she said, "Now you will be disappointed, for instead of telling you to come and study with me, or go and act in some second-rate theater at once, I advise you to go back to school and finish your education. That is the first step, for all accomplishments are needed, and a single talent makes a very imperfect character. Cultivate mind and body, heart and soul, and make yourself an intelligent, graceful, beautiful and healthy girl. Then, at eighteen or twenty, go into training and try your powers. We have to climb slowly, with many slips. Can you wait as well as work?"

"I will!"

"We shall see. It would be pleasant to me to know that when I quit the stage I leave behind me a well-trained, faithful, gifted comrade to more than fill my place. But remember, mere beauty and costumes do not make an actress. Cultivate that talent of yours. It is a special gift, this power to bring tears and smiles, and it is a sweeter task to touch the heart than to freeze the blood or fire the imagination."

"That's what Uncle Laurie says; and he and Aunt Jo try to plan plays about true and lovely things—simple domestic scenes that touch people's hearts, and make them laugh and cry and feel better."

"Tell your uncle he is right, and ask your aunt to try a play for you. I'll come and see it when you are ready."

"Will you? Oh! will you? We are going to have some at Christmas, with a nice part for me. A simple little thing, but I can do it, and should be so proud, so happy, to have you there."

Josie rose as she spoke, for a glance at the clock showed her that her visit was a long one; and hard as it was to end this momentous interview, she felt that she must go. Catching up her hat she went to Miss Cameron, and said, "I can never thank you enough for this hour and all you have told me. I shall do just as you advise, and mamma will be very glad to see me settled at my books again. I can study now with all my heart, because it is to help me on; and I won't hope too much, but work and wait, and try to please you, as the only way to pay my debt."

"That reminds me that I have not paid mine. Little

friend, wear this for my sake. It is fit for a mermaid, and will remind you of your first dive. May the next bring up a better jewel." As she spoke, Miss Cameron took from the lace at her throat a pretty pin of aquamarine, and fastened it on Josie's chest; then lifting the happy little face, she kissed it very tenderly, and watched it go smiling away.

6. The Worm Turns

One September afternoon, two brown and dusty bicyclists went whirling up the road to Plumfield.

"Go ahead and report your news, Tom; I'm due here. See you later," said Demi, swinging himself down at the door of the Dovecote.

"Yes, here I go to have it out with Mother Bhaer," said Thomas Bangs. He had a story which would, he thought, astonish and dismay everyone.

To his great joy Mrs. Jo was discovered alone in a pile of proofsheets for her new book. She dropped the sheets to greet the returning wanderer. But after the first glance she saw that something was the matter. "What is it now, Tom?" she asked.

"I'm in an awful scrape, ma'am."

"Of course; I'm always prepared for scrapes when you appear. What is it? You ran over some old lady who is going to sue you?"

"Worse than that," groaned Tom.

"Not poisoned some trusting soul who asked you to prescribe him something, I hope?"

"Worse than that."

"You haven't let Demi catch a horrible disease and left him behind, have you?"

"Worse even than that."

"I give up. So tell me."

"I'm engaged!"

59

Mrs. Jo exclaimed in dismay, "If Nan has yielded to your badgering, I'll never forgive her!"

Tom laughed, "She hasn't. It's another girl."

"I'm glad, very glad indeed! Then I don't care who it is; and I hope you'll be married soon. Now tell me all about it."

"But what will Nan say?"

"She will be rejoiced to be rid of the mosquito who has pestered her so long. Don't worry about Nan. Who is this 'other girl'?"

"Demi hasn't written you about her?"

"Only something about your upsetting some Miss West."

"That was only the beginning of a series of scrapes. Just my luck! Of course, after what I did to the poor girl I had to be attentive to her, hadn't I? Everyone seemed to think so, and I couldn't get away, and so I was lost before I knew it. It's all Demi's fault; he had to stay there and fuss with his photographing, because all the girls wanted to get their pictures taken. Look at these shots, will you, ma'am? That's the way we spent our time when we weren't playing tennis." And Tom pulled a handful of pictures from his pocket, displaying several in which he was very prominent, either holding a parasol over a very pretty young lady on the rocks, lying at her feet in the grass or perched on a piazza railing with other couples in bathing costumes.

"This is *she,* of course?" asked Mrs. Jo.

"That's Dora. Isn't she lovely?"

"Very nice little person to look at."

"She's very smart, too. She can keep house, and sew, and do lots of things, I assure you, ma'am. All the girls like her, and she's sweet-tempered and jolly, and sings like a bird, and dances beautifully, and loves books. She thinks yours are splendid, and made me talk about you no end."

Jo laughed. "That last sentence is to flatter me and win my help to get you out of your scrape. Tell me first how you got in it."

"Well, she and I had met before, but I didn't know she was there. Demi wanted to see a friend, so we went, and finding it nice and cool rested over Sunday. We found some pleasant people and went out rowing. I had Dora, and in almost no time cracked up the boat on a rock. She could swim, no harm done, only she got scared and had her gown spoiled. She took it well, and we got friendly at once—couldn't help it, scrambling into that beast of a boat while the rest laughed at us. Of course we had to stay another day to see that Dora was all right. Demi wanted to. Alice Heath is down there and two other girls from our college, so we sort of lingered along, and Demi kept taking pictures, and we danced, and got into a tennis tournament. That fact is, tennis is a dangerous game, ma'am. A great deal of courting goes on on those courts."

"Not much tennis in my day, Tom, but I understand perfectly."

"Upon my word, I hadn't the least idea of being serious, but everyone else was flirting, so I did. Dora seemed to like it and expect it, and of course I was glad to be agreeable. She thought I was somebody, though Nan does not, and it was pleasant to be appreciated after years of being snubbed. Yes, it was jolly to have a sweet girl smile at you all day, and blush prettily when you said a funny thing to her, and look glad when you came, sorry when you left, and admire all you did, and make you feel like a man and act your best. That's the sort of treatment a fellow enjoys and ought to get if he behaves himself; not frowns and cold shoulders year in and year out, and made to look like a fool when he means well, and is faithful, and has loved a girl ever since he was a boy. No, by Jove, it's not fair, and I won't stand it!"

"I wouldn't," said Mrs. Jo. "Drop your old fancy for Nan—for it's nothing more than a fancy—and take up the new one. But how came you to propose, Tom, as you must have done to be engaged?"

"Oh, that was an accident. I didn't mean it at all; the

donkey did it, and I couldn't get out of the scrape without
hurting Dora's feelings, you see," began Tom.

"So there were two donkeys in it, were there?" said Mrs.
Jo, foreseeing fun of some sort.

"Don't laugh! It sounds funny, I know; but it might have
been awful," answered Tom. "The girls admired our bikes,
and of course we liked to show off. We took 'em for rides,
and had a good time generally. Well, one day Dora was on
behind me, and we were going nicely along a good bit of
road, when a ridiculous old donkey got right across the
way. I thought he'd move, but he didn't, so I gave him a
kick; he kicked back, and over we went in a heap, donkey
and all. Such a mess! I thought only of Dora, and she had
hysterics; at least, she laughed till she cried, and that
beast brayed, and I lost my head. Any fellow would, with
a poor girl gasping in the road, and he wiping her tears
and begging pardon, not knowing whether her bones were
broken or not. I called her my darling, and went on like a
fool, till she grew calmer, and said, with such a look, 'I forgive you, Tom. Pick me up, and let us go on again.'

"Wasn't that sweet now, after I'd upset her for the second time? It touched me to the heart; and I said I'd like to
go on forever with such an angel to steer for, and—well, I
don't know what I did say; but you might have knocked
me down with a feather when she put her arm around my
neck and whispered, 'Tom, dear, with you I'm not afraid of
any lions in the path.' She might have said *donkeys*; but
she meant it. And now here I am with two sweethearts on
my hands!"

"Tommy Bangs! Who but you could ever get into such a
scrape?" laughed Mrs. Jo.

"Isn't it a mess, and won't everyone tease me to death
about it? I shall have to get out of town for a while."

"No, indeed; I'll stand by you, for I think it is the best
joke of the season. But tell me how things ended. Is it really serious, or only a summer flirtation?"

"Well, Dora considers herself engaged, and wrote to her
folks at once. I couldn't say a word when she took it all

like that and seemed so happy. She's only seventeen, never liked anyone before, and is sure all will be fine; that is, her father knows mine, and we are both well off. I was so staggered that I said, 'Why, you can't love me really when we know so little of one another?' But she answered right out of her tender little heart, 'Yes, I do, dearly, Tom; you are so good and kind and honest, I couldn't help it.' Now, after that, what could I do but go ahead and make her happy while I stayed, and trust to luck and time to straighten it all out?"

"A truly Tom Bangsian way of dealing with matters! I hope you told your father at once?"

"Oh, yes, I wrote right off and broke it to him in three lines. I said, 'Dear Father, I'm engaged to Dora West, and I hope she will suit the family. She suits me tip-top. Yours ever, Tom.' He was all right, never liked Nan, you know; but Dora will suit him down to the ground."

"What did Demi say to this?" asked Mrs. Jo.

"He was immensely interested and very kind; talked to me like a father; said it was a good thing, only I must be honest with her and myself and not trifle a moment. Demi is quite a wiseman, especially when he is in the same boat."

"You don't mean—?" gasped Mrs. Jo.

"Yes, I do, ma'am. He *said* he went to Quitno to see Fred Wallace, but he never saw the fellow. How could he, when Wallace was off in his yacht all the time we were there? Alice Heath was the real attraction, and I was left to my fate. There were three donkeys on this trip, and I'm not the worst one. Demi will look innocent, and no one will say a word to him."

"The midsummer madness has broken out," remarked Mrs. Jo, "and no one knows who will be crazed next. Well, leave Demi to his mother, and let us see what you are going to do, Tom."

"I don't know exactly; it's awkward to be in love with two girls at once. What do you advise?"

"Common sense. Dora loves you and thinks you love

her. Nan does not care for you, and you only care for her as a friend, though you have tried for so much more. It is my opinion, Tom, that you love Dora, or are on your way to it; for in all these years I've never seen you look or speak about Nan as you do about Dora. Nan's nay-saying has made you cling to her till chance has shown you a more attractive girl. Now, I think you had better take the old love as a friend, the new one as a sweetheart, and in due time, if the feeling is genuine, marry her."

Tom's eyes shone, his lips smiled, and a new expression of happiness glorified him.

"The fact is," he told his motherly friend, "I meant to make Nan jealous, for she knows Dora, and I was sure she would hear of our doings. I was tired of being walked on, and I thought I'd try to break away and not be a laughing-stock any more. I was astonished to find it so easy and so pleasant. I didn't mean to do any harm, but drifted along, and told Demi to mention things in his letters to Daisy, so Nan might hear of it. Then I forgot Nan altogether, and saw, heard, felt, cared for no one but Dora, till the donkey—bless his old heart!—tossed her into my arms, and I found she loved me. Upon my soul, I don' t see why she should! I'm not half good enough."

"Every honest man feels that when a beloved girl puts her hand in his. Make yourself worthy of her, for she isn't an angel but a woman with faults of her own for you to bear and forgive, and you must help one another," said Mrs. Jo.

"What troubles me is that I didn't mean it when I began, and was going to use the dear girl to help me torture Nan. It wasn't right, and I don't deserve to be so happy. If all my scrapes ended as well as this, what a state of bliss I should be in!" And Tom beamed again.

"My dear boy, it is not a scrape, but a very sweet experience suddenly dawning upon you," answered Mrs. Jo. "Enjoy it wisely and be worthy of it, for it is a serious thing to accept a girl's love and trust, and let her look up to you for tenderness and truth in return. Be a man in all things for Dora's sake, and make this affection a blessing to you both."

"I'll try! Yes, I do love her, only I can't believe it just yet. Wish you knew her. Dear little soul, I long to see her already! She cried when we parted last night, and I hated to go.—I declare, I feel as if a weight was off me, but what the dickens will Nan say when she knows it!"

"Knows what?" asked a clear voice that made both start and turn, for there was Nan calmly looking them over from the doorway.

Anxious to put Tom out of suspense and to see how Nan would take the news, Mrs. Jo answered quickly, "Tom's engagement to Dora West."

"Really?" and Nan looked so surprised that Mrs. Jo was afraid she might be fonder of her old playmate than she knew; but her next words set the fear at rest, and made everything comfortable and merry at once.

"Dear old Tom, I'm so glad. Bless you!" And she shook both his hands with hearty affection.

"It was an accident, Nan. I didn't mean to, but I'm always getting into messes, and I couldn't seem to get out of this any other way. Mother Bhaer will tell you all about it. I must go and make myself tidy. Going to tea with Demi. See you later."

Tom suddenly bolted, leaving the elder lady to enlighten the younger.

After Mrs. Jo explained, Nan remarked, "I shall miss him of course, but it will be a relief to me and better for him. Now he will go into business with his father and do well, and everyone be happy."

"And now you can give your whole mind to your work," said Mrs. Jo; "for you are fitted for your profession, and will be an honor to it by and by."

"I hope so. That reminds me—measles are in the village, and you had better tell the girls not to call where there are children. It would be bad to have a run of them. Now I'm off to Daisy." And Nan departed, happy for her friend Tom.

Though one swallow does not make a summer, one en-

gagement is apt to make several, and Jo's boys were, most
of them, at the inflammable age when a spark ignites the
flame that soon flickers and dies out, or burns warm and
clear for life. Nothing could be done about it but for Mrs.
Jo to help them make wise choices and be worthy of good
mates. But of all the lessons she had tried to teach her
boys, this great one was the hardest; for love is apt to
make lunatics of even saints and wisemen, so young people cannot be expected to escape the delusions, disap-
pointments and mistakes, as well as the delights, of this
sweet madness.

"I suppose there is no helping it, but I hope that some
of the new ideas of education will produce a few hearty,
happy and intelligent girls for my lads. Lucky for me that
I haven't the whole twelve on my hands. I should lose my
wits if I had, for I foresee troubles ahead worse than Tom's
donkeys and Doras," thought Jo.

"Mother, can I have a little serious conversation with
you?" asked Demi one evening, as they sat together enjoying the first fire of the season, while Daisy wrote letters upstairs and Josie was studying in the little library close by.

"Certainly, dear. No bad news, I hope?" And Mrs. Meg
looked up from her sewing with a mixture of pleasure and
anxiety.

"It will be good news to you, I think," answered Demi,
who had no intention of telling of his flirtation with Alice.
"I know you don't like my being a reporter, and will be
glad to hear that I have given the job up."

"I am very glad! It is too uncertain a business. I want
you settled in some good place where you can stay."

"What do you say to a railroad office?"

"I don't like it. A noisy kind of place, with all sorts of
rough men about. I hope it isn't that, dear?"

"How does a travelling salesman suit you?"

"Not at all."

"I could be a private secretary to a writer; but the salary
is small, and may end any time."

"That would be better, but I don't want my son to spend his best years grubbing for a little money in a dark office. I want to see you in some busines where your talents can be developed. I talked it all over with your dear father when you were a child, and if he had lived, he would have shown you what I mean, and helped you to be what he was."

Demi put his arm round her now, as he said, in a voice so like his father's that it was the sweetest music to her ear, "Mother dear, I think I have got just what you want for me. I didn't say anything till it was sure, because it would only worry you; but Aunt Jo and I have been on the lookout for it some time, and now it has come. You know her publisher, Mr. Tiber, who is so generous and kind? Well, I've hankered after a job there; for I love books, and as I can't write them I'd like to help publish them. The atmosphere at Mr. Tiber's is so different from the dark offices and hurly-burly of other trades, where nothing but money is talked about, and I feel at home in it."

"Just what I should like, dear! Have you got it? Your career is made if you go to that well-established place, with those good men to help you along!"

"I think I have got it; but I'm only on trial, and must begin at the bottom and work my way up. Mr. Tiber will push me on as fast as I prove myself fit to go up. I'm to begin the first of next month in the book-room, filling orders; and I go round and get orders, and do various other things of the sort. I am ready to do anything about books, if it's only to dust them," laughed Demi.

"You inherit that love of books from Grandpa; he can't live without them. I'm glad of it. Books are a comfort all one's life. I am truly glad and grateful, John, that at last you want to settle down, and have got such an entirely satisfactory place. Do your best, and be as honest, useful and happy as your father."

"I'll try, mother. Mr. Tiber said, 'This is only to teach you the ropes, Brooke; I shall have other work for you by and by.' Aunty told him I had done book reviews, and had rather a fancy for literature. I know it is a very honorable profession to select and give good books to the world; and I'm satisfied to be a humble helper in the work."

"I'm glad you feel so. It adds so much to one's happiness to love the task one does. I used to hate teaching; but housekeeping for my own family was always sweet, though much harder in many ways. Isn't Aunt Jo pleased about all this?" asked Mrs. Meg.

"So pleased that I could hardly keep her from letting the cat out of the bag too soon."

"It is a happy day for me. Now I am at ease about you. If only Daisy can be happy, and Josie give up her dream of acting, I shall be quite contented."

"Why not have a great actress in our family, as well as an author, a minister and an important publisher?" said Demi. "We don't choose our talents. I say, let Josie have her own way and Daisy be happy in her way."

"I don't see but I must, if I could only feel that such lives would not hurt the girls. I suppose if your blessed father had not come along, I'm afraid I myself should have been an actress."

7. Emil's Thanksgiving

The *Brenda* was scudding along with all sails set to catch the rising wind, and everyone on board was rejoicing, for the long voyage was drawing toward an end.

"Four weeks more, Mrs. Hardy, and we'll give you a cup of tea such as you never had before," said second mate Emil Hoffmann, as he paused beside two ladies sitting in a sheltered corner of the back deck.

"I shall be glad to get it, and still gladder to put my feet on solid ground," answered the elder lady, smiling; for our friend Emil was a favorite; since he devoted himself to the captain's wife and daughter, who were the only passengers on board.

"So shall I. I've tramped up and down the deck so much, I shall be barefooted if we don't arrive soon," laughed Mary, the daughter, showing two shabby little boots as she glanced up at the companion of these tramps, remembering gratefully how pleasant he had made them.

"I don't know what you would have done for exercise, dear, if Mr. Hoffmann had not made you walk every day. This lazy life is bad for young people, though it suits an old body like me well enough in calm weather."

"Please sing, Mr. Hoffmann," said Mary, "it's so pleasant to have your music. We shall miss it very much when we get ashore."

Leaning on the rail near the girl, he watched her brown locks blowing in the wind as he sang her favorite song:

"Give me a freshening breeze, my boys,
A white and swelling sail,
A ship that cuts the dashing waves,
And weathers every gale.
What life is like a sailor's life,
So free, so bold, so brave?
His home the ocean's wide expanse,
A coral bed his grave."

Just as the last notes of the clear, strong voice died away, Mrs. Hardy suddenly exclaimed, "What's that?"

Emil's quick eye saw at once the little puff of smoke coming up a hatchway where no smoke should be, and his heart seemed to stand still for an instant as the dread word "Fire!" flashed through his mind. Then he was quite steady, so as not to alarm the women, and strolled away, saying quietly, "Smoking not allowed there, I'll go and stop it." But the instant he was out of sight he leaped down that hatchway, thinking, "If we are on fire, I shouldn't wonder if I did make 'a coral bed my grave.'"

He was gone a few minutes, and when he came up, choking with smoke, he went to report to the captain: "Fire in the hold, sir."

"Don't frighten the women," was Captain Hardy's first order.

In spite of the streams of water poured into the hold over the smoking cargo, it was soon evident that the ship was doomed. Smoke began to ooze up between the planks, and the rising gale soon fanned the smoldering fire to flames that began to break out here and there, telling the dreadful truth too plainly for anyone to hide. Mrs. Hardy and Mary bore the shock bravely when told to be ready to leave the ship at a moment's notice; the lifeboats were hastily prepared, and the men worked with a will to batten down every loophole from which the fire might escape. Soon the poor *Brenda* was a floating furnace, and the order to "Take to the boats!" came for all. The women first, of course, but their boat lingered near, for the brave captain would be the last to leave the ship.

Emil stayed by him till ordered off; but it was well for him he went, for just as he had got in the boat, a mast fell with a crash, knocking Captain Hardy overboard. The lifeboat soon reached him as he floated out from the wreck, and Emil sprung into the sea to rescue him, for he was wounded and unconscious. This accident made it necessary for Emil to take command, and he at once ordered the men to row for their lives, as an explosion might occur at any moment.

The other boats were out of danger and all lingered to watch the splendid but terrible sight of the burning ship alone on the wide sea, reddening the night sky and then slowly settling to her watery grave. No one saw the end, however, for the gale soon swept the watchers far away and separated them, some never to meet again in this life.

The boat containing the women, the captain, Emil and seven other sailors was all alone when dawn came up. Food and water had been put in, but it was evident that with a badly wounded man, two women and seven sailors their supply would not last long, and help was sorely needed. Their only hope was in meeting a ship, although the gale, which had raged all night, had blown them out of their course. They whiled away the weary hours watching the horizon.

Second mate Hoffmann was very brave and helpful, though this unexpected responsibility weighed heavily on his shoulders. The first day and night passed in comparative comfort, but when the third came, things looked dark and hope began to fail. Captain Hardy was raving, his wife worn out, the girl weak for want of food, having put away half her biscuit for her mother and given her share of water to wet her father's feverish lips. The sailors stopped rowing and sat grimly waiting. All day Emil tried to cheer and comfort them, while hunger gnawed at him and growing fear lay heavy at his heart. He told stories to the men, implored them to bear up for the helpless women's sake and promised rewards if they would row while they had strength to regain the lost route, and increase their chance of rescue. He rigged a tent of sailcloth over the suffering captain and comforted the wife, and tried to make the pale girl forget the danger by singing every song he knew.

The fourth day came and the supply of food and water was nearly gone. Emil proposed to keep it for the sick man and the women, but two of the men rebelled, demanding their share. Emil gave up his own as an example, and several of the good fellows followed it. During the night, while Emil, worn out, left the watch to the most trustworthy sailor that he might snatch an hour's sleep, the two selfish sailors got at the supplies and stole the last of the bread and water, and the one bottle of brandy. Half mad with thirst, they drank greedily and by morning one was passed out, from which condition he never awoke; and the other was so crazed by the brandy that when Emil tried to control him he fell overboard and was lost.

Another trial came to them that left all of them more despairing than before. A sail appeared, and for a time a frenzy of joy came over them, to be turned to the bitterest disappointment when it passed by, too far away to see the signals waved to them or hear the frantic cries for help that rang across the sea. Emil's heart sunk then, for the captain seemed to be dying, and the women could not hold out much longer. He kept a strong face on it till night came; then in the darkness, Emil hid his face and wept. It was not the pain that broke him, but his dreadful powerlessness to conquer the cruel fate that seemed hanging over them. If he could only save these dear and innocent women from death, he felt that he could willingly give his life for them.

As he sat there with his head in his hands, Emil thought of his happy past at Plumfield. His talk on the housetop with Aunt Jo seemed but yesterday, and he thought, "The red strand! I must remember it, and do my duty to the end. If you can't come into port, old boy, go down with all sail set."

A sail appeared, and for a time a frenzy of joy came over them.

A sudden shout startled him, and a drop on his fore-head told him that the blessed rain had come at last, bringing salvation with it; for thirst is harder to bear than hunger, heat or cold. Welcomed by cries of joy, all lifted up their parched lips, held out their hands and spread their garments to catch the great drops that soon came pouring down to cool the sick man's fever, quench the agony of thirst and bring refreshment to every weary body in the boat. All night it fell, all night the castaways revelled in the saving shower, and took heart again, like dying plants revived by heaven's dew. The clouds broke away at dawn, and Emil sprung up, wonderfully cheered. But this was not all: as his eye swept the horizon, clear against the rosy sky shone the white sails of a ship, so near that they could see the pennants on her masthead and black figures moving on the deck.

One cry broke from all, as every man waved hat or handkerchief and the women stretched their hands to-wards this white angel. Answering signals from the ship assured them of help; and in the joy of that moment the happy women fell on Emil's neck. He always said that was the proudest moment of his life, as he stood there holding Mary in his arms; for the brave girl clung to him half-fainting.

When all were safely aboard the good *Urania,* home-ward bound, Emil told the story of the wreck before he thought of his own needs. Nearly fainting at the smell of soup, he asked, "What day is this?"

Frank William, the ship's surgeon, answered, "Thanks-giving Day! And we'll give you a regular New England din-ner, if you'll eat it."

But Emil was too worn out to do anything, except lie still and give thanks for the blessed gift of life.

8. Dan's Christmas

Where was Dan? In prison. Alas for Mrs. Jo! How her heart would have ached if she had known that while old Plumfield shone with Christmas cheer her boy sat alone in his cell, trying to read the little book she gave him. Yes, Dan was in prison; but no cry for help came from him; for his own sin had brought him there, and this was to be the bitter lesson that tamed the lawless spirit and taught him self-control.

The story of his downfall is soon told; for it came, as so often happens, just when he felt unusually full of high hopes, good resolutions and dreams of a better life. On his journey he met a pleasant young fellow, and naturally felt an interest in him, as Blair was on his way to join his elder brothers on a ranch in Kansas. Card-playing was going on in one of the cars of the train, and the lad—for he was barely twenty—tired with the long journey, spent his time with any who passed through. Dan, true to his promise not to gamble, would not join in, but watched with intense interest the games that went on, and soon made up his mind that two of the men were card-sharpers anxious to fleece the boy. Dan always had a soft spot for any younger, weaker creature whom he met, and something about the lad reminded him of Teddy; so he kept an eye on Blair, and warned him against his new friends.

Vainly, of course; for when all stopped overnight in one of the great cities of the West, Dan missed the boy from the hotel where he had taken him for safe-keeping; and learning who had come for him, went to find him, unable to leave the trusting boy to the dangers that surrounded him.

He found him gambling in a low-down place with the men, who were determined to get his money; and by the look of relief on Blair's anxious face when he saw him, Dan knew that things were going badly.

"I can't come yet—I've lost; and it's not my money; I must get it back, or I dare not face my brothers," whispered the poor lad, when Dan begged him to get away without further loss. But the boy played on, sure that he could recover the money entrusted to his care.

Dan kept watch of every card till he plainly detected false play, and boldly said so. Strong words passed, Dan's anger overcame his wisdom; and when the cheat refused to restore the boy's money and insulted Dan and pulled out a gun, Dan's hot temper flashed out, and he knocked the man down with a blow that sent him crashing head-first against a stove, to roll unconscious and bleeding to the floor. A wild scene followed, but in the middle of it, Dan whispered to the boy, "Get away, and don't say a word. Don't worry about me."

Frightened and confused, Blair left the city at once, leaving Dan to pass the night in jail, and a few days later to stand in court charged with manslaughter; for the man was dead. Dan had no friends there, and having once briefly told his story, held his peace, anxious to keep all knowledge of this sad affair from those back home. He even concealed his name—giving it as David Kent, as he had done several times before in emergencies. His sentence was a year in prison, with hard labor.

Dan knew that a letter would bring Mr. Laurie to help him; but he could not bear to tell of this disgrace, or see the sorrow and the shame it would cause the friends who hoped so much for him.

"No," he said, clenching his fists, "I'll let them think me dead first. I shall be if I am kept here long." He paced the stone floor like a caged lion till he felt as if he should go mad and beat upon the walls.

The warden of this prison was a harsh man, but the chaplain, Garvy Michaels, was full of sympathy, and did his hard duty faithfully and tenderly. Mr. Michaels labored with poor Dan, but seemed to make no impression, and was forced to wait till labor had soothed Dan's anger and captivity had tamed his energy.

Dan did his daily task, ate his bitter bread and obeyed commands with a rebellious flash of the eye, which made the warden say, "That's a dangerous man. Watch him. He'll try to break out some day."

There were others more dangerous than he, and these men soon divined Dan's mood, and managed to tell him before a month was over that plans were being made for a break-out at the first chance. Thanksgiving Day was one of the few times for them to speak together as they enjoyed an hour of freedom in the prison yard. Then all would be settled and the rash attempt made, probably to end in bloodshed and defeat for most, but liberty for a few. Dan had already planned his own escape, but was growing more moody, fierce and rebellious. He brooded over his ruined life, gave up all his happy hopes and plans, felt that he could never face dear old Plumfield again or touch those friendly hands with the stain of blood on his own. He did not care for the wretched man whom he had killed, but the disgrace of prison would never be wiped out of his memory.

"It's all over with me; I've spoiled my life. I'll give up the fight and get what pleasure I can. They shall think me dead and so still care for me, but never know what I am. Poor Mother Bhaer! She tried to help me, but it's no use. The firebrand can't be saved."

The Sunday before Thanksgiving, as he sat in chapel, Dan observed several guests in the seats reserved for them. People often came to speak to the convicts, so it did not surprise him when, on being invited to address them, one of the ladies rose and said she would tell them a little story.

The speaker was a middle-aged woman in black, with a

kind face and eyes, and a voice that seemed to warm the heart. She reminded Dan of Mrs. Jo, and he listened intently to every word, feeling that each was meant for him. It was a very simple story, but it caught the men's attention at once, being about two soldiers in a hospital during the Civil War, both badly wounded in the right arm, and both anxious to save these limbs and go home unmaimed. One patient cheerfully obeyed orders, even when told that the arm must go. After much suffering he recovered, grateful for life, though he could fight no more. The other rebelled, would listen to no advice and, having delayed too long, died a lingering death, bitterly regretting his folly when it was too late.

"Now, as all stories should have a little moral," said the woman, "let me tell you mine. This prison is a hospital for soldiers wounded in life's battle; here are sick souls, weak wills and insane passions bringing with them their pain and punishment. There is hope and help for everyone, for God's mercy is infinite and man's charity is great; but sorrow for our wrongs and submission to our punishments must come before the cure is possible. Pay the penalty manfully, for it is just; but from the suffering and shame wring new strength for a nobler life. The scar will remain, but it is better for a man to lose both arms than his soul; and these hard years, instead of being lost, may be made the most precious of your lives, if they teach you to rule yourselves. O friends, try to wash the sin away, and begin anew. If not for your own sakes, for that of the dear mothers, wives and children who wait and hope so patiently for you."

There the little sermon ended; but the preacher of it felt her words had not been uttered in vain, for one boy's head was down, and several faces wore the softened look that told that a tender memory was touched.

Dan was forced to set his lips to keep them steady, and lower his eyes to hide the sudden dew that dimmed them. He was glad to be alone in his cell again, and sat thinking deeply, instead of trying to forget himself in sleep. It seemed as if those words were just what he needed to show him where he stood and how fateful the next few days might be to him. Should he join the "bad lot," and perhaps add another crime to the one already committed, and destroy the future that might yet be redeemed? Or should he submit, bear the punishment, try to be the better for it?

Good and evil fought for Dan that night, and it was hard to tell whether lawless nature or loving heart would conquer. In the dark hour before the dawn, as he lay wakeful on his bed, a ray of light shone through the bars, the bolts turned softly and a man came in. It was the good chaplain.

"I have bad news," said Mr. Michaels. "Your friend, the old man named Mason, in the cell next door, has died. He left a message for you."

"Thank you, sir, I'd like to hear it."

"He went suddenly, but remembered you, and begged me to say these words, 'Tell him not to do it, but to hold on, do his best, and when his time is out go right to Mary, my wife, and she'll make him welcome for my sake. He was kind to me, and Mary and God will bless him for it.' Then he died quietly."

Dan said nothing, but laid his arm across his face and lay quite still.

"I hope you won't disappoint this humble friend whose last thought was for you. Keep up your courage, son, and go out at the year's end better, not worse. Let us ask God to help you as only He can."

After that visit, there was a change in Dan, though no one knew it but the chaplain; for to all the rest he was the same silent, stern, unsocial fellow as before, and turning his back on the bad and the good alike, found his only pleasure in the books he had brought from Mrs. Jo's home.

At Christmas he yearned so for Plumfield that he devised a way to send a word of greeting to cheer their anxious hearts. He wrote to Mary, Mason's widow, who lived in another state, asking her to mail the letter he enclosed.

In it he merely said he was well and busy, had given up the farm, and had other plans which he would tell later; he would not be home before fall probably, nor write often, but was all right, and sent love and Merry Christmas to everyone.

Then he took up his solitary life again, and tried to take his punishment manfully.

"I don't expect to hear from Emil yet, and Nat writes regularly, but where is Dan? Only two or three notes since he went. Such an energetic fellow as he is could buy up all the farms in Kansas by this time," said Mrs. Jo one morning when the mail came in and no card or envelope bore Dan's dashing hand.

"He never writes often, you know, but does his work and then comes home. Months and years seem to mean little to him, and he is probably prospecting in the wilderness, forgetful of time," answered Mr. Bhaer.

"But he promised he would let me know how he got on, and Dan keeps his word if he can. I'm afraid something has happened to him."

"Don't worry, Mum dear," said Teddy, "nothing ever happens to the old fellow. He'll turn up all right, and come stalking in some day with a gold mine in one pocket and a prairie in the other."

"Perhaps he has gone to Montana and given up the farm plan. He seemed to like the Indians best, I thought," said Rob.

"I hope so, it would suit him best. But I am sure he would have told us his change of plan and sent for some money to work with. No, I feel in my bones that something is wrong," said Mrs. Jo.

"Then we shall hear; bad news travels fast," said Mr. Bhaer. "Don't meet trouble halfway, Jo, but listen to this letter from Nat and how well he is getting on." Nat had written of parties he had been to, the splendors of the Leipsic opera, the kindness of his new friends, the delight of studying violin under such a great master as Schott, his hopes of rapid improvement and his great gratitude to those who had opened this enchanted world to him.

"That, now, is satisfactory," said Mrs. Jo. "I felt that Nat had unsuspected power in him before he went away; he was so manly and full of excellent plans."

"We shall see," said Professor Bhaer. "He will doubtless get his lessons from the world. That comes to us all in our young days."

9. Waiting

"My wife, I have bad news for you," said Mr. Bhaer, coming in one day early in January.

"Please tell it at once. I can't bear to wait, Fritz," cried Mrs. Jo, dropping her work and standing up.

"But we must wait and hope, heart's dearest. Come and let us bear it together. Emil's ship is lost, and as yet no news of him."

It was a good thing Mr. Bhaer had taken his wife into his strong arms, for she looked ready to drop, but bore up after a moment, and sitting by her good man, heard all that there was to tell. Tidings had been sent to the shipowners at Hamburg by some of the survivors, and telegraphed at once by Franz to his uncle Fritz. As one boat-load from the ship was safe, there was hope that others might also escape, though the gale had sent two to the bottom. A swift-sailing steamer had brought this scanty news, and happier news might come at any hour. But kind Franz had *not* added that the sailors reported the captain's boat as undoubtedly wrecked by the falling mast, since the smoke hid its escape, and the gale soon drove all far apart. In time the sad rumor of captain's wrecked boat did reach Plumfield; and deep was the mourning for the happy-hearted Commodore, never to come singing home again.

Mrs. Jo refused to believe it, stoutly insisting that Emil would outlive any storm and yet turn up safe and cheerful. It was good she clung to this hopeful view, for poor Mr.

Bhaer was much afflicted by the loss of his nephew, because his sister's sons had been his so long he scarcely knew a different love for his very own.

Little Josie, Emil's pet cousin, was so broken-hearted, nothing could comfort her. To cry in mother's arms and talk about the wreck, which haunted her even in her sleep, was all she cared to do, and Mrs. Meg was anxious about her until Miss Cameron sent Josie a kind note bidding her learn bravely her first lesson in real tragedy, and *be* like the self-sacrificing heroines she loved to *act*. That did the girl good, and she made an effort.

As Emil was helping nurse Captain Hardy, safe and well aboard the steamer, all this sorrow would seem wasted; but it was not, for it drew many hearts more closely together by a common grief, taught some of them patience, some sympathy, some regret for faults that lie heavy on the conscience when the one sinned against is gone, and all of them the lesson to be ready when our time to die comes. A hush lay over Plumfield for weeks, and Emil's flag hung at half-mast on the roof where he last sat with Mrs. Jo.

So the weeks went heavily by till suddenly, like a thunderbolt out of a clear sky, came the news, "All safe, letters on the way." Then up went the flag, out rang the college bells, bang went Teddy's long-unused cannon and a chorus of happy voices cried, "Thank God," as people went about laughing, crying and embracing one another in delight. By and by the longed-for letters came, and all the story of the wreck was told; briefly by Emil, at length by Mrs. Hardy, gratefully by the captain, while Mary added a few tender words that went straight to their hearts and seemed the sweetest of all. Never were letters so read, passed round, admired and cried over as these; for Mrs. Jo carried them in her pocket when Mr. Bhaer did not have them in his, and both took a look at them when they said their prayers at night. Now the professor was heard humming like a big bee again as he went to his classes, and the lines smoothed out of Mother Bhaer's forehead,

while she wrote this story to anxious friends and let her
novel wait. Best of all, little Josie lifted up her head and
began to bloom again, growing tall and quiet.

Now another sort of waiting began; for the travellers
were on their way to Hamburg, and would stay there
awhile before coming home, as Uncle Hermann owned the
Brenda, and the captain must report to him. Emil must remain for Franz's wedding. These plans were welcome and
pleasant after the troublous times which went before.

There was great scrubbing and dusting by each family
as they set their houses in order not only for Graduation
Day, but to receive the bride and groom, who were to
come to them for the honeymoon trip. Great plans were
made, gifts prepared and much joy felt at the thought of
seeing Franz again; though Emil, who was to accompany
them, would be the greater hero.

Dan, in the meantime, was also counting the weeks till
August, when he would be free. But neither marriage-bells
nor festival music awaited him; no friends would greet
him as he left the prison; no hopeful prospects lay before
him; no happy homecoming was to be his. Yet his success
was great, though only God and Garvy Michaels, the chaplain, saw it. It was a hard-won battle; but he would never
have to fight so terrible a one again. Soon he was to be
free again, out among men in the blessed sun and air.
Night after night he lulled himself to sleep with planning
how, when he had seen Mary Mason according to his
promise, he would steer straight for his old friends, the Indians, and in the wilderness hide his disgrace. Working to
save the many would atone for the sin of killing one, he
thought; and the old free life would keep him safe from the
temptations that faced him in the cities.

"By and by, when I'm all right again, and have something to tell that I'm not ashamed of, I'll go home," he said.
"Not yet. I must get over this first. They'd see and smell
and feel the prison on me, if I went now, and I couldn't
look them in the face and hide the truth. I can't lose Ted's

love, Mother Bhaer's trust, and the respect of—of—the girls—for they did respect me; but now they wouldn't. I'll make 'em proud of me yet; and no one shall ever know of this awful year. I *can* wipe it out, and I will, so help me God!"

10. Jo's Girls

Although this story is about Jo's boys, her girls cannot be neglected, because they held a high place in this little world of the college, and special care was taken to fit them to play their parts in the larger world that offered them wider opportunities and more serious duties.

At Laurence College all found something to help them; for the growing institution had not yet made its rules too fixed, and believed so heartily in the right of all sexes, colors and creeds to education that there was room for everyone who knocked, and a welcome to the awkward youths from up country, the eager girls from the West, the freedman or woman from the South or the well-born student whose poverty made this college a possibility when other doors were barred. There still was prejudice, ridicule, neglect in high places and prophecies of failure to contend against; but the faculty was composed of cheerful, hopeful men and women.

Among the various customs which had very naturally sprung up was one especially useful and interesting to "the girls," as the young women liked to be called. It all grew out of the sewing hour still kept by the three sisters. Meg, Jo and Amy were busy women, yet on Saturdays they tried to meet in one of the three houses. With books and work, their daughters by them, they read and sewed and talked in the sweet privacy that women love, and can make so helpful.

Mrs. Meg was the first to propose enlarging this little

circle; for as she went her motherly rounds among the
young women students she found a sad lack of order and
skill in domestic education. Latin, Greek, mathematics
and science of all sorts went well; but sewing went un-
heeded. Anxious lest the usual sneer at learned women
who can't take care of a household should apply to "our
girls," she gently lured two or three of the most untidy
young women to her house, and made the hour so pleasant that they were grateful for the favor, and asked to
come again. Others soon begged to join the party, and
soon it was a privilege so much desired that the need for
more space came: the boys and girls' old museum was re-
fitted with sewing-machines, tables, rocking chairs and a
cheerful fireplace, so that, rain or shine, the sewing nee-
dles might go on mending.

One day a brisk discussion arose concerning careers
for women. Mrs. Jo had read something on the subject
and asked each of the dozen girls sitting about the room
what she intended to do on leaving college. The answers
were as usual: "I shall teach"; "I shall help mother"; "I shall
study medicine . . . art . . ."; but nearly all ended with, "till
I marry."

"But if you don't marry, what then?" asked Mrs. Jo.

"Be old maids, I suppose," answered a lively lass.

"Old maids aren't sneered at half as much as they used
to be, since some of them have grown famous and proved
that woman isn't a half but a whole human being, and can
stand alone," said Mrs. Jo. "It is well to consider the fact,
and fit yourselves to be useful women."

"I don't like the thought of being an old maid, all the
same," said a plain girl. "We can't all be heroines like Miss
Cobbe, Miss Nightingale and Miss Phelps. So what can we
do but sit in a corner and watch life pass us by?"

"Cultivate cheerfulness and content, if nothing else. But
there are so many little odd jobs waiting to be done that
nobody need 'sit idle and look on' unless she chooses,"
said Mrs. Meg with a smile.

"One of the best and most beloved women I know has

been doing odd jobs for the Lord for years, and will keep at it till her dear hands are folded in her coffin," remarked Mrs. Jo. "All sorts of things she does—picks up neglected children and puts them in safe homes, saves lost girls, nurses poor women in trouble, sews, knits, begs, works for the poor people day after day with no reward but the thanks of them she helps. That's a life worth living; and I think that the quiet little woman will get a higher seat in Heaven than many of those of whom the world has heard."

"I know it's lovely, Mrs. Bhaer; but it's dull for young folks. We do want a little fun before we get down to such work," said a Western girl.

"Have your fun, my dear; but if you must earn your bread, try to make it sweet with cheerfulness, not bitter with the daily regret that it isn't cake. I used to think mine was a very hard fate because I had to amuse a somewhat fretful old lady; but the books I read in that library have been of immense use to me since, and the dear old soul left me Plumfield for my 'cheerful service and affectionate care.' I didn't deserve it, but I did use to try to be jolly and kind, and get as much honey out of duty as I could, thanks to my dear mother's help and advice."

"Gracious! If I could earn a place like this, I'd sing all day and be an angel. But you have to take your chances, and get nothing for your pains, perhaps. I never do," said the Westerner.

"Don't do it for the reward; but be sure it will come, though not in the shape you expect. I worked hard for fame and money one winter; but I got neither, and was much disappointed. A year afterward I found I had earned two prizes: skill with my pen, and—Professor Bhaer!"

Mrs. Jo's laugh was echoed by the girls, who liked to have these conversations enlivened by illustrations from life.

"You are a very lucky woman," began one discontented young lady.

"Yet her nickname used to be 'Luckless Jo,' and she never had what she wanted till she had given up hoping for it," said Mrs. Meg.

"I'll give up hoping, then, right away, and see if my wishes will come," said the discontent. "I only want to help my folks, and get a job teaching at a good school."

A pretty one said, "I think I should like being a spinster, on the whole—they are so independent. My Aunt Jenny can do just what she likes, and ask no one's permission; but Ma has to consult Pa about everything."

"No one objects to women doing plenty of domestic work or having too much fashionable pleasure," said a stately girl. "But the minute we begin to study, people tell us we can't bear it, and warn us to be very careful. I tried other things, and got so tired I came to college. And now I'm stronger in body, and much happier in mind. I think I was dying of boredom."

"That active brain of yours was dying for good food," said Mrs. Meg. "It has plenty now, and plain living suits you better than luxury. It is all nonsense about girls not being able to study as well as boys. Neither can bear cramming. We will prove to you that wise head-work is a better cure for 'delicacy' than medicine. Too many girls burn the candle at both ends; and when they break down, they blame the books, not the parties and balls."

"Dr. Nan was telling me about a patient of hers who thought she had a weak heart," said Mrs. Jo. "Then Nan made her take off her corsets, stop drinking coffee and dancing all night, and made her eat, sleep and walk regularly for a time; and now she's 'cured.'"

"I've had no headaches since I came here, and can do twice as much studying as I did at home. It's the air, I think, and the fun of getting ahead of the boys," said another girl, tapping her forehead with a thimble.

At the end of the afternoon, the girls trooped away with their work-baskets, feeling that though they might never be Elizabeth Brownings or George Eliots, they might become noble, useful and independent women, and earn for themselves some sweet title from the grateful lips of the poor, better than any a queen could bestow.

An especially lovely graduation day came round, bringing the usual roses, strawberries, white-gowned girls, beaming youths, proud friends and stately dignitaries. As Laurence College was a mixed one, the presence of young women as students gave to the occasion a grace and animation entirely wanting where women appear merely as spectators.

College Hill, Parnassus and old Plum swarmed with cheery faces, as guests, students and professors hurried to and fro in the pleasant excitement of arriving and receiving. Everyone was welcomed cordially, whether he rolled up in a fine carriage or trudged on foot to see the good son or daughter come to honor on the happy day that rewarded many sacrifices. Mr. Laurie and his wife were on the reception committee, and their lovely house was overflowing. Mrs. Meg, with Daisy and Josie as helpers, was in demand among the girl graduates, helping with dressing and fitting and decorating. Mrs. Jo had her hands full as the college president's wife, and as the mother of Ted; for it took all the power and skill of that energetic woman to get her son into his Sunday best.

Professor Bhaer was a proud and happy man when, at the appointed hour, he looked down upon the youthful faces before him, thinking of the "little gardens" in which he had hopefully and faithfully sowed good seed years ago, and from which this beautiful harvest seemed to have sprung. Mr. March's fine old face shone with satisfaction, for this was the dream of his life fulfilled after patient waiting. Laurie always kept himself out of the way as much as courtesy would permit on these occasions; for everyone spoke gratefully in speech and poem of the founder of this college. The three sisters, meanwhile, beamed with pride as they sat among the ladies, enjoying the honor done the men they loved.

The music was excellent; the poems were—as usual on such occasions—of varied excellence, as the youthful speakers tried to put old truth into new words, and made them forceful by the enthusiasm of their earnest faces and fresh voices. It was beautiful to see the eager interest with which the girls listened to some brilliant brother-student, and applauded him; it was still more pleasant to watch the young men's faces when a slender white figure stood against the background of black-coated dignitaries, and with cheeks that flushed and paled, and lips that trembled, spoke to them straight out of woman's heart and brain concerning the hopes and doubts, the aspirations and rewards all must know and labor for. This clear, sweet voice seemed to reach and rouse all that was noblest in the souls of these youths, and to set a seal upon the years of comradeship which made them sacred and memorable forever.

Alice Heath's speech was unanimously pronounced the success of the day; for without being flowery, it was sensible and so inspiring that she left the stage in a storm of applause, the good fellows being much fired by her stirring appeal to "march shoulder to shoulder." Demi was so excited that he nearly rushed out of his seat to hug her as she hastened to hide herself among her mates, who welcomed her with faces full of pride and tearful eyes. A prudent Daisy stopped him, however, and in a moment he was able to listen distractedly to uncle Fritz's presidential remarks.

Mr. Bhaer spoke like a father to the children whom he was dismissing to the battle of life; and his tender, wise and helpful words lingered in their hearts.

Food and refreshment took up the rest of the afternoon, and at sunset came the beginning of the evening's festivities. There was much strolling, singing and flirting.

The appearance of a very dusty vehicle loaded with trunks at Mr. Bhaer's door was a surprise to onlookers, especially as two rather foreign-looking gentlemen sprung out, followed by two young ladies, all four being greeted with cries of joy and much embracing by the Bhaers. Who were these mysterious strangers, wondered the guests. One female student declared that they must be the professor's nephews, one of whom was expected on his honeymoon.

All four were greeted with cries of joy.

She was right. Franz proudly presented his blonde bride to his aunt and uncle, and within a moment of her being kissed and welcomed, Emil led up his Mary, with the announcement, "Uncle, Aunt Jo, here's another daughter! Have you room for *my* wife, too?"

There could be no doubt of that; and Mary was embraced by her new relatives, who, remembering all the young pair had suffered together, felt that this was the natural and happy ending of the long voyage so perilously begun.

"But why didn't you tell us before, and let us be ready for two brides instead of one?" asked Mrs. Jo.

"Well, I remembered what a good joke you all considered Uncle Laurie's marriage, and I thought I'd give you another nice little surprise," laughed Emil. "I'm off duty, and it seemed best to take advantage of wind and tide, and come along. We hoped to get in last night, but couldn't do it, so here we are in time for the end of the graduation anyway."

"Ah, my sons," said Mr. Bhaer, with tears rolling down his cheeks, "it is too feeling-full to see you both so happy and again in the old home. I have no words to outpour my gratitude, and can only ask of the dear God in Heaven to bless and keep you all."

And then of course everyone began to talk—Franz and his bride Ludmilla in German with the uncle, Emil and Mary with the aunts; and round this group gathered the young folk, clamoring to hear all about the shipwreck, and the rescue and the homeward voyage. It was a very different story from the written one; and they listened to Emil's words, with Mary's soft voice breaking in now and then to add some fact that brought out the courage and patience he so lightly touched upon.

"I never hear the patter of rain now that I don't want to say my prayers; and as for women, I'd like to take my hat off to every one of 'em, for they are braver than any man I ever saw," said Emil.

"If women are brave," said Mary, "some men are as

tender and self-sacrificing as women. I know one who in
the night slipped his share of food into a girl's pocket,
though starving himself, and sat for hours rocking a sick
man in his arms that he might get a little sleep. No, love, I
will tell, and you must let me!" cried Mary, holding in both
her own the hand he laid on her lips to silence her.

"Only did my duty," said Emil. "If that torment had
lasted much longer I might have been as bad as the poor
souls who got drunk and died that night."

"Don't think of that, dear. Tell about the happy days on
the *Urania,* when Papa grew better and we were all safe
and homeward bound," said Mary.

Emil, sitting with his arm about his "dear lass," in true
sailor fashion told the happy ending of the tale.

"Such a jolly old time as we had at Hamburg. Uncle Hermann couldn't do enough for the captain, and while
Mamma took care of him, Mary looked after me. I had to
go into dock for repairs! Fire hurt my eyes, and watching
for a sail and want of sleep made 'em as hazy as a London
fog. She was pilot and brought me in all right, you see,
only I couldn't part company with her, so she came
aboard as first mate of my life."

"Hush! That's silly, dear," whispered Mary.

"The captain proposed waiting a spell before marrying,
but I told him we weren't likely to see any rougher
weather than we'd pulled through together, and if we
didn't know one another after such a year as this, we
never should. So I had my way, and my brave little woman
has shipped for the long voyage. God bless her!"

"Shall you really sail with him?" asked Daisy.

"I'm not afraid," answered Mary. "I've seen my captain
in fair weather and in foul, and if he is ever wrecked again,
I'd rather be with him than waiting and watching from
ashore."

"A true woman, and a born sailor's wife! You are a
happy man, Emil, and I'm sure *this* trip of marriage will be
a prosperous one," cried Mrs. Jo. "Oh, my dear boy, I always felt you'd come back, and when everyone else de-

spaired I never gave up, but insisted you were clinging to the main-top jib somewhere on that dreadful sea." Mrs. Jo grasped Emil and hugged him.

"Of course I was!" answered Emil. "And my 'main-top jib' was the thought of what you and uncle said to me. That kept me up; and among the million thoughts that came to me during those lonely nights none was clearer than the idea of the red strand, you remember—the English navy, and all that. I liked the notion, and resolved that if a bit of my cable was left afloat, the red stripe should be there."

"And it was, my dear, it was!—Captain Hardy testifies to that, and Mary here is your reward." And Mrs. Jo kissed Emil's bride with a maternal tenderness.

Soon Emil and his bride were borne away to feast on the cookies he desired, and Mrs. Jo and Meg joined the other group, glad to hear what Franz was saying about Nat.

"Nat will get fine training," Franz was explaining, "in Bachmeister's orchestra, and also see London. If he works out, he'll be a fixture among the violins. 'Tell Daisy,' he said, 'and be sure to tell her all about my success.' I'll leave that to you, Aunt Meg, and you can also break it gently to her that the old boy has a fine blond beard. It's very becoming. Ludmilla has a photo of him for you."

They listened to many other interesting bits of news which Franz had not forgotten to remember for his friend's sake. He talked well, and painted for them Nat's hard work so vividly that Mrs. Meg was half won over to his side, and already imagined herself telling Daisy, "All right; your boy has done well; be happy, dear."

11. Life for Life

The summer days that followed were full of rest and pleasure for young and old, as they showed Plumfield to their happy guests. While Franz and Emil were busy with the affairs of Uncle Hermann and Captain Hardy, Mary and Ludmilla made friends everywhere; for, though very unlike, both were excellent and charming girls. Mrs. Meg and Daisy found the German bride a housewife after their own hearts, and had delightful times learning new dishes and discussing domestic life in all its branches. Ludmilla not only taught, but learned, many things, and went home with many new and useful ideas in her pretty head.

Mary had seen so much of the world that she was unusually lively for an English girl. Mrs. Jo was quite satisfied with Emil's choice, and felt sure this woman would bring him safe to port through fair or stormy weather. Jo felt at rest about these boys, and enjoyed their visit with real, maternal satisfaction; she parted with them in September most regretfully, yet hopefully, as they sailed away to the new life that lay before them.

Demi, meanwhile, had become engaged to Alice Heath, but they kept the engagement quiet, for both were too young to do anything but love and wait. They were so happy that time seemed to stand still for them, and after a blissful week they parted bravely—Alice to home duties, and John to his business at the publisher's in Boston, full of a new goal, saving enough money to wed.

Daisy rejoiced over them, and was never tired of hearing her brother's plans for the future. Her own hope, marrying Nat, soon made her what she used to be—a cheery, busy creature, with a smile, kind word and helping hand for all; and as she went singing through the house again, her mother felt that the right remedy for past sadness had been found.

And as for Josie, she had a month of acting lessons with Miss Cameron at the seaside. She threw herself heartily into the lessons that were of infinite value to her in the busy, brilliant years to come; for Josie's talents were to blossom, and by and by she would become a famous and beloved actress.

Tom and his Dora were on their slow and easy way to the altar. Dora was a most devoted and adoring little mate, and made life so pleasant to him that his gift for getting into scrapes seemed lost, and he seemed on his way to becoming a thriving businessman.

Mrs. Jo was beginning to think her trials were over for that year when a new excitement came. Several postcards had arrived at long intervals from Dan, who gave them "Care of M. Mason" as his address. By this means he was able to gratify his longing for home news, and to send brief messages to quiet their surprise at his delay in settling down. The last one, which came in September, was dated "Montana," and simply said, "Here at last, trying mining again; but not going to stay long. All sorts of luck. Gave up the farm idea. Tell plans soon. Well, busy and very happy.—D.K."

They didn't know that Dan was "very happy" because he was *free*! Meeting an old friend by accident, he took a job as overseer for a time, finding the company even of rough miners very sweet, and the work pleasant, after being cooped up in jail so long. He longed to go home, but waited week after week to get the look of prison off him. Meanwhile he made friends of workers and bosses; and as no one knew his story, he took his place again in the world.

One October day, Ted came rushing in to his mother, with a newspaper in his hands. "Mine caved in!" he panted. "Twenty men—no way out—wives crying—water rising—Dan knew the old shaft—risked his life—got 'em out—most killed—papers full of it—I knew he'd be a hero—hurrah for old Dan!"

"What? Where? When? Who? Stop roaring, Teddy, and let me read!" commanded his mother, entirely bewildered.

Very proud were all who soon read the account of how Daniel Kean was the one who, in the first panic of the accident, remembered the old shaft that led into the mine—walled up, but the only hope of escape, if the men could be got out before the rising water drowned them; how he was lowered down alone, telling the others to keep back till he saw if it was safe; how he heard the poor fellows picking desperately for their lives on the other side, and by knocks and calls guided them to the right spot; then he headed the rescue party, and working like a hero, got the men out in time. On being drawn up last of all, the worn ropes broke, and he had a terrible fall, being much hurt, but still alive. The owners of the mine promised him a handsome reward, if he lived to receive it!

"He must live; he shall, and come home to be nursed as soon as he can move, if I have to go and bring him back myself! I always knew he'd do something fine and brave, if he didn't get shot or hung for some prank instead," cried Mrs. Jo.

"Do go, and take me with you, Mum," said Teddy. "I ought to be the one, Dan's so fond of me and I of him."

Before his mother could reply, Mr. Laurie came in, with almost as much noise and flurry as Teddy, exclaiming, "Seen the news, Jo? What do you think? Shall I go off at once and see after that brave boy?"

"I wish you would."

"Then I'll go at once. If he's able, I'll bring him home; if not, I'll stay and see to him. He'll pull through. Dan will never die of a fall on his head. He's got nine lives, and not lost half of them yet."

"I've never seen such a year, with wrecks and weddings and floods and engagements, and every sort of catastrophe!" exclaimed Mrs. Jo.

"If you deal in boys and girls, you must expect this sort of thing, ma'am. The worst is over, I hope, till these lads of your own begin to go off," laughed Mr. Laurie. "But now I'll be off."

Mr. Laurie went, and Teddy rode into town with him, vainly asking to be taken along to his Dan.

From out West, Laurie soon sent letters. Dan was very ill; he did not recognize his friend for several days. Then he began to mend, and cheering accounts soon followed. At length Dan was pronounced able to travel, but he seemed in no haste to go home.

"Dan is strangely altered," Laurie wrote to Jo. "It is not by this illness alone, but by something which has evidently happened before. I don't know what, but from his ravings when delirious I fear he has been in some serious trouble this past year. He seems ten years older, but improved, quieter and so grateful to us. He says Kansas was a failure, but he can't talk much. The people here love him very much; he wants everyone to think well of him, and can't do enough to win affection and respect."

Mrs. Jo wrote Dan and begged him to come home; she spent more time in composing a letter that should bring him than she did over the most thrilling episodes in her "works."

No one but Dan saw this letter; but it did bring him, and one November day Mr. Laurie helped a feeble man out of a carriage at the door of Plumfield, and Mother Bhaer received the wanderer like a recovered son.

"Right upstairs and rest; I'm nurse now, and this ghost must eat before he talks to anyone," commanded Mrs. Jo.

Dan was quite content to obey, and lay on the lounge in the room prepared for him, looking like a sick child restored to its own nursery and mother's arms, while his new nurse fed him, bravely controlling the questions that burned upon her tongue. Being weak and weary, he soon fell asleep; and then she stole away.

"Jo, I think Dan has committed some crime and suffered for it," said Mr. Laurie. "Some terrible experience has come to the lad, and broken his spirit. In his delirium he spoke of 'the warden,' some trial, a dead man, and would keep offering me his hand, asking me if I would take it and forgive him. Once, when he was very wild, I held his arms, and he quieted in a moment, imploring me not 'to put the handcuffs on.' I declare, it was quite awful sometimes to hear him in the night talk of old Plum and you, and beg to be let out and go home to die."

"He isn't going to die, but live to repent of anything he may have done," said Jo with tears in her eyes. "I don't care if he's broken the Ten Commandments, I'll stand by him, and so will you, and we'll set him on his feet and make a good man of him yet. Don't say a word to anyone of this, and I'll have the truth from him before long."

For some days Dan rested, and saw few people; then good care, cheerful surroundings, and the comfort of being at home began to tell, and he seemed more like himself, though still silent as to his late experiences. Ted was much disappointed that he could not show off his brave Dan.

"Wasn't a man there who wouldn't have done the same, so why make a fuss over me?" asked the hero.

"But isn't it pleasant to think that you saved twenty lives, Dan, and gave husbands, sons and fathers back to women who loved them?" asked Mrs. Jo one evening when they were alone.

"Pleasant! It's all that kept me alive, I do believe; yes, I'd rather have done it than been made president. No one knows what a comfort it is to think I've saved twenty men to more than pay for—" There Dan stopped short.

"It is a splendid thing to save life at the risk of one's own," began Mrs. Jo.

"'He that loseth his life shall gain it,'" muttered Dan.

"Then you *did* read the little book I gave you?" said Mrs. Jo.

"I read it a good deal after a while."

"Oh, my dear, tell me about it! I know something lies heavy on your heart; let me help you bear it, and so make your burden lighter."

"I know it would; I want to tell; but some things even you couldn't forgive; and if *you* let go of me, I'm afraid I can't keep afloat."

"Mothers can forgive anything! Tell me all, and be sure that I will never let you go, though the whole world should turn from you."

Mrs. Jo took one of his big hands in both of hers and held it fast, waiting silently till that touch warmed poor Dan's heart, and gave him courage to speak. With his head in his hands, he slowly told it all, never once looking up till the last words left his lips.

"Now you know; can you forgive a murderer, and keep a jail-bird in your house?"

Her only answer was to put her arms about him, and lay his head on her breast, with eyes so full of tears they could but dimly see.

That was better than any words; and poor Dan clung to her in speechless gratitude, feeling the blessedness of mother love—that divine gift which comforts and strengthens all who seek it.

"My poor boy, how you have suffered all this year, when we thought you free as air! Why didn't you tell us, Dan, and let us help you?"

"I was ashamed. I tried to bear it alone rather than shock and disappoint you, as I know I have, though you try not to show it." And Dan's eyes dropped again as if they could not bear to see the dismay his confession painted on his best friend's face.

"I am shocked and disappointed by the sin, but I am also very glad and proud and grateful that my sinner has repented, and is ready to profit by the bitter lesson. No one but Fritz and Laurie need ever know the truth; we owe it to them, and they will feel as I do."

"No, they won't; men never forgive like women. But it's all right. Please tell 'em for me, and get it over with. Mr.

Laurie must know it already; I blabbed when my wits were dizzy; but he was very kind all the same. I can bear their knowing it; but, oh, not Ted and the girls!" Dan clutched her arm with such an imploring face that she hastened to assure him no one should know except the two old friends, and he calmed down.

"It wasn't murder, mind you, it was in self-defence," explained Dan. "He drew first, and I had to hit him. Didn't mean to kill him; but it doesn't worry me as much as it ought, I'm afraid. I've more than paid for it, and such a rascal is better out of the world than in it, showing boys the way to hell. Yes, I know you think that's awful of me; but I can't help it. I hate a scoundrel as I do a skulking coyote, and always want to get a shot at 'em. Perhaps it would have been better if he had killed me; my life is spoiled."

All the old prison gloom seemed to settle like a black cloud on Dan's face as he spoke, and Mrs. Jo was frightened at the glimpse it gave her of the fire through which he had passed to come out alive, but scarred for life. Hoping to turn his mind to happier things, she said, "No, it isn't; you have learned to value it more and use it better. It is not a lost year, but one that may prove the most helpful of any you ever know. Try to think so, and begin again; we will help."

"I never can be what I was. I feel about sixty, and don't care for anything now I've got here. Let me stay till I'm on my legs, then I'll clear out and never trouble you any more."

"You are weak and low in your mind; that will pass, and by and by you will go to your missionary work among the Indians with all the old energy and the new patience, self-control and knowledge you have gained. Tell me more about that good chaplain and Mary Mason and the lady whose chance word helped you so much. I want to know all about the troubles of my poor boy."

Won by her tender interest, Dan brightened up and talked on till he had poured out all the story of that bitter year, and felt the better for the load he lifted off.

If he had known how it weighed upon his hearer's heart, he would have held his peace; but she hid her sorrow till she had sent him to bed, comforted and calm; then she cried her heart out, to the great dismay of Fritz and Laurie, till they heard the tale and could mourn with her; after which they all took counsel together how best to help this worst of all the "catastrophes" the year had brought them.

It was curious to see the change which came over Dan after that talk. A weight seemed off his mind; he seemed intent on showing his gratitude and love to these true friends by a new humility. After hearing the story from Mrs. Jo, the professor and Mr. Laurie made no allusion to it beyond the hearty handshake, the look of compassion, the brief word of good cheer in which men express sympathy. Mr. Laurie began at once to interest influential persons in Dan's mission to the Indians. Mr. Bhaer gave Dan's hungry mind something to do, and helped him understand himself by carrying on the prison chaplain's task. The boys took him out on drives, while the women, old and young, nursed and cared for him till he felt like a sultan.

Daisy cooked for him; Nan attended to his medicines; Josie read aloud to him to help him pass the long hours he needed on the couch; while Bess brought all her pictures and sculptures to amuse him, and, at his special desire, set up a modelling-stand in the parlor and began to sculpt the buffalo head he had given her. Those afternoons seemed the pleasantest part of his day; and Mrs. Jo, busy in her study close by, could see the friendly trio. He often called Josie "little mother," but Bess was always "Princess"; and his manner to the two cousins was quite different. Josie sometimes fretted him with her fussy ways, the long plays she liked to read and the maternal scoldings she liked to give. To Bess, he never showed either impatience or weariness, but obeyed her least word.

Mrs. Jo warned Teddy not to trouble Dan with

questions till he was quite well; but Dan's approaching departure made the boy resolve to have a full, clear and satisfactory account of the adventures which he felt sure must have been thrilling. So one day when the coast was clear, Ted volunteered to amuse the patient, and did so in the following manner: "Look here, old boy, if you don't want me to read to you, you've got to talk, and tell me all about Kansas, and the farms, and that part. The Montana business I know, but you seem to forget what went before. Brace up, and let's have it."

"No, I don't forget; it isn't very interesting to anyone but myself. I didn't see any farms—I gave it up."

"Why?"

"Other things to do."

"What?"

"Well, brush-making for one thing."

"Don't tease me. Tell me the truth."

"I truly did."

"What for?"

"To keep out of trouble."

"Well, of all the strange things—and you've done a lot—that's the strangest," cried Ted. "But what trouble, Dan?"

"Never you mind."

"But I do want to know, awfully, because I'm your pal, and care for you. I always have. Come on now, tell me a good story. I love hearing about fights. I'll be mum as an oyster if you don't want it known."

"Will you?" and Dan looked at him, wondering how the boyish face would change if the truth were suddenly told him.

"I'll swear I won't tell anyone, if you like. I know it must have been a great fight, and I'm aching to hear."

"You're as curious as a girl! Josie and Bess never asked me such questions."

"They don't care about fights and things; they liked the mine business, heroes and all that. So do I, and I'm as proud as punch over it; but I see by your eyes that there was something else before that, and I'm bound to find out

Ted volunteered to amuse the patient.

who Blair and Mason are, and who was hit and who ran away, and all the rest of it."

"What!"

"Well, when you first got here you used to mutter about 'em in your sleep, and I wondered. But never mind, if you can't remember, or would rather not."

"What else did I say? Strange, what stuff a man will talk when his wits are gone."

"That's all I heard; but it seemed interesting, and I just mentioned it, thinking it might refresh your memory a bit," said Teddy.

Dan wiped a frown off his face, and made up his mind to amuse Ted with some half-truths, hoping to quench his curiosity, and so get peace.

"Let me see; Blair was a lad I met on the train; and Mason a poor fellow who was in a—a sort a hospital where I happened to be. Blair ran off to his brothers, and I suppose I might say Mason was hit, because he died there. Is that enough?"

"No, it isn't. Why did Blair run? And who hit the other fellow? I'm sure there was a fight somewhere, wasn't there?"

"Yes."

"I guess I know what it was about."

"The devil you do! Let's hear you guess."

Ted at once unfolded his boyish solution to the mystery. "You needn't say yes, if I guess right and you are under oath to keep silent. I shall know by your face, and never tell. Out there they have wild doings, and it's my belief you were in some of 'em. I don't mean robbing the mail and that sort of thing; but defending the settlers, or hanging some scamp, or even shooting a few, as a fellow must sometimes, in self-defence. Ah, ha! I've hit it, I see. You needn't speak; I know the flash of your old eye."

"Drive on, smart boy, and don't lose the trail," said Dan.

"I knew I should get it; you can't deceive me for long," began Ted.

Dan could not help a short laugh.

"It's a relief, isn't it, to have it off your mind?" asked Ted. "Now just tell me the rest, unless you've sworn not to tell."

"I have."

"Oh, well, then don't.—I guess I understand. I'm glad you stood by your friend in the hospital. How many did you kill?"

"Only one."

"A bad one?"

"A damned rascal."

"Well, I've no objection. I wouldn't mind popping at some of those bloodthirsty crooks myself. You had to hide and keep quiet after it, I suppose."

"Pretty quiet for a long spell."

"Got off all right in the end, and headed for your mines and did that jolly brave thing. Now I call that all decidedly interesting. I'm glad to know it; but I won't blab."

"Mind you don't. Look here, Ted, if you'd killed a man, would it trouble you—a bad one, I mean?"

"Well, if it was my duty in war or self-defence, I suppose I shouldn't; but if I'd pitched into him in a rage, I guess I should be very sorry. Shouldn't wonder if he sort of haunted me. You don't have that on your conscience, do you? It was a fair fight, wasn't it?"

"Yes, I was in the right; but I wish it hadn't happened.— Now mind you keep your notions to yourself, for some of 'em are wide of the mark. You may read aloud now if you like." And there the talk ended; but Ted took great comfort in it.

A few quiet weeks followed, during which Dan became more and more eager to be off and live for others, since he might not live for himself.

So one wild March morning he rode away with his horse and hound, to face again the enemies inside himself who would have conquered him but for Heaven's help and human kindness.

"Ah, me! It does seem as if life was made of partings, and they get harder as we go on," sighed Mrs. Jo.

It is a strong temptation to the weary novelist to close the present story with an earthquake which would engulf Plumfield so deeply in the depths of the earth that no archeologist could ever find a trace of it. But as that somewhat heavy-handed conclusion might shock my gentle readers, I will refrain, and cut off the need for the usual question of "How did they end up?" by briefly stating all the marriages turned out well. The boys prospered in their various careers; so did the girls, for Bess and Josie won honors in their artistic careers, and in the course of time found worthy husbands. Nan remained a busy, cheerful, independent spinster, and dedicated her life to her suffering friends and their children, in which true woman's work she found continuing happiness.

Dan never married, but lived, bravely and usefully, among his chosen people till he was shot defending them, and at last lay quietly asleep in the green wilderness he loved so well, with a smile on his face which seemed to say that he had fought his last fight and was at peace. Demi became a partner in the publishing firm, and lived to see his name above the door. Rob became a professor at Laurence College, following his father's footsteps; but Teddy eclipsed them all by becoming a famous and eloquent clergyman, to the great delight of his astonished mother.

And now, having tried to suit everyone by many weddings, few deaths and as much prosperity as life permits, let the music stop, the lights die out and the curtain fall forever on the March family.